Donald MacKenzie and The Murder Room

>>> This title is part of The Murder Room, our series dedicated to making available out-of-print or hard-to-find titles by classic crime writers.

Crime fiction has always held up a mirror to society. The Victorians were fascinated by sensational murder and the emerging science of detection; now we are obsessed with the forensic detail of violent death. And no other genre has so captivated and enthralled readers.

Vast troves of classic crime writing have for a long time been unavailable to all but the most dedicated frequenters of second-hand bookshops. The advent of digital publishing means that we are now able to bring you the backlists of a huge range of titles by classic and contemporary crime writers, some of which have been out of print for decades.

From the genteel amateur private eyes of the Golden Age and the femmes fatales of pulp fiction, to the morally ambiguous hard-boiled detectives of mid twentieth-century America and their descendants who walk our twenty-first century streets, The Murder Room has it all. >>>

The Murder Room
Where Criminal Minds Meet

themurderroom.com

Donald MacKenzie 1908–1994

Donald MacKenzie was born in Ontario, Canada, and educated in England, Canada and Switzerland. For twenty-five years MacKenzie lived by crime in many countries. 'I went to jail,' he wrote, 'if not with depressing regularity, too often for my liking.' His last sentences were five years in the United States and three years in England, running consecutively. He began writing and selling stories when in American jail. 'I try to do exactly as I like as often as possible and I don't think I'm either psychopathic, a wayward boy, a problem of our time, a charming rogue. Or ever was.'

He had a wife, Estrela, and a daughter, and they divided their time between England, Portugal, Spain and Austria.

By Donald MacKenzie

Henry Chalice

Salute from a Dead Man (1966)
Death is a Friend (1967)
Sleep is for the Rich (1971)

John Raven

Zaleski's Percentage (1974)
Raven in Flight (1976)
Raven and the Ratcatcher
  (1976)
Raven and the Kamikaze (1977)
Raven After Dark (1979)
Raven Settles a Score (1979)
Raven and the Paperhangers
  (1980)
Raven's Revenge (1982)
Raven's Longest Night (1983)
Raven's Shadow (1984)
Nobody Here By That Name
  (1986)
A Savage State of Grace (1988)
By Any Illegal Means (1989)
Loose Cannon (1994)
The Eyes of the Goat (1992)
The Sixth Deadly Sin (1993)

Standalone novels

Nowhere to Go (1956)
The Juryman (1957)
The Scent of Danger (1958)
Dangerous Silence (1960)
Knife Edge (1961)
The Genial Stranger (1962)
Double Exposure (1963)
The Lonely Side of the River
  (1964)
Cool Sleeps Balaban (1964)
Dead Straight (1968)
Three Minus Two (1968)
Night Boat from Puerto
  Vedra (1970)
The Kyle Contract (1971)
Postscript to a Dead Letter
  (1973)
The Spreewald Collection
  (1975)
Deep, Dark and Dead (1978)
The Last of the Boatriders
  (1981)

Death is a Friend

Donald MacKenzie

An Orion book

Copyright © The Estate of Donald MacKenzie 1967

The right of Donald MacKenzie to be identified as the author of this work has been asserted in accordance with the Copyright, Designs and Patents Act 1988.

This edition published by
The Orion Publishing Group Ltd
Orion House
5 Upper St Martin's Lane
London WC2H 9EA

An Hachette UK company
A CIP catalogue record for this book is available from the British Library

ISBN 978 1 4719 0493 6

www.orionbooks.co.uk

For Estrela with love

BRUCE CAMERON

8th November

NIGHT RAIN bombarded the roof of the parked station wagon and ran deep in the gutters. He kept his eyes on the windshield, peering through the space cleared by the wipers. The rubber blades squeaked monotonously. The man sitting behind the wheel turned his wrist and checked a stopwatch. His pipe glowed, the light revealing a narrow head with a thin nose and lips and sparse sandy hair. The tone of his voice added a touch of pedantry — well bred and unemotional like that of a youngish don.

"Any moment now."

Cameron wound his window down another couple of inches. Half an hour in a closed car with Thorne's pipe was more effective than the lung cancer warnings of an entire medical family. He grunted skeptically.

"You've said that three times."

His accent was Canadian with a prairie drawl. He pushed fingers through shortish black hair shot with gray over the ears. His inch-long sideburns were completely white. He shifted in his seat when Thorne made no answer.

1

"Didn't you hear what I said — who are you trying to convince?"

Thorne took his pipe out of his mouth. He knocked the bowl into the ashtray.

"Nobody," he said quietly. "Use your imagination. You're a company secretary earning two thousand a year. Married but no kids to claim income tax relief on. Your wife complains that she doesn't see enough life. A letter arrives at your flat. In it you find a couple of tickets for a show half London is trying to see. The note enclosed says 'Enjoy yourselves and think of us.' No signature and you don't recognize the handwriting. What do *you* do — return the tickets to the theater?" He shook his head, smiling faintly.

Cameron was still watching the apartment block, a four-wing building with a pretentious portico at the main entrance. The stonework was discolored and the paint needed renewing. As far as he could see there was no one on duty in the lobby. Far off on the left, blurred lights signaled the seedy joys of Edgeware Road. He shrugged.

"I'll *tell* you what I'd do. I'd sit behind my front door with a chair leg, waiting to clobber the guy who sent the tickets."

Thorne polished his signet ring on his trousers. "That's because you've got a particular sort of mind. These people don't think like that. They haven't anything to lose. If the woman owns any jewelry, she'll be wearing it all tonight. I can see it already. A string of cultured pearls and a half-hoop of synthetic sapphires. You're forgetting that she wants to *live*, Bruce. And front-row stalls is living. Apart from all . . ."

He broke off, grabbing the binoculars in his lap. He trained them on the glass-domed entrance then gave them to Cameron. The Canadian refocussed, pulling the scene within touching distance. Two people were standing just inside the revolving door. The woman's hair was bound in a scarf. She had what looked like a fur cape round her shoulders. The man holding her arm wore spectacles and a dinner jacket. A cab drove by the parked car and drew up in front of the entrance to the lobby. The couple hurried down the steps, the man holding an umbrella over the woman's head. The cab drove off, spraying water across the forecourt.

Cameron put the binoculars down. The familiar feeling tightened his stomach, a mixture of guilt and excitement. He fastened the belt on his raincoat.

"OK. Give me the gear."

Thorne dropped a key into his outstretched palm, added a pencil-sized flashlight. He spoke as if he were summarizing a lengthy lecture.

"Leave things as you find them. Don't touch anything unnecessarily. Be extra careful about things like rugs — vases. Women notice. I'll move the car under the window in twenty minutes. If you need me you know what to do."

He indicated the telephone booth on the sidewalk. The sign they had hung on it glistened in the rain.

OUT OF ORDER

3

Cameron pulled on a pair of thin pigskin gloves. He snapped the flashlight on and off experimentally.

"If anything goes wrong," he said, "don't start hollering. You're the expert — not me."

Thorne had his pipe going again. He sucked hard on the stem before answering.

"Nothing'll *go* wrong. Take my word for it."

Cameron turned his coat collar up round his chin. He ducked into the beating rain. His rubber soles made wet tracks across the linoleum in the dimly lit side entrance. The small elevator was self-operated. He rode it to the top floor. The corridor was empty. He walked past the smell of frying fish to a door with an initialed mat before it. The brass mailbox was brightly polished. Above it was a bellpush.

He hesitated, drawn to put his thumb on the bell — half hoping that if he did the door would be thrown open by someone Thorne hadn't counted on. A friend, maybe, who'd come in to watch television. He'd smile — give them something about a wrong number then go down and bawl the hell out of Henry.

He pushed the skeleton key firmly into the mortise lock and turned it. The door opened just the way Thorne had said it would — straight out of the Burglar's Manual. He stepped into warm darkness and locked himself in. He shone the flash round the narrow hallway. They'd gone over the layout of the small apartment so often that it was fixed in his brain. Straight ahead was the bedroom. The outside wall enclosed the living room. Kitchen and bathroom were on the left. Noises from the neighboring apartments filtered through the thin partition walls. A child screaming; someone scraping a fiddle; a persistent cough. The tiny beam traveled over the coats hanging on the hallstand. He tried the pockets of the blue Helton. They held only bus tickets. He moved past a ticking grandfather clock, poised on the tips of his toes.

The sitting room door was ajar. He went through without touching it. The floor was covered with a fluffy gray carpet. Everything but the desk bore the mark of mediocrity. Chintz sofa covers — fake-Swedish chairs — a few run-of-the-mill prints. The desk was old and dwarfed the room. A portrait of its owners stood on top — the woman in a bridal gown and train, dotted with confetti — the man in a cutaway coat, holding his top hat like a receptacle. None of the drawers was locked. He pulled one out after another, feeling under the neatly stacked correspondence. Nothing there either. He picked up a briefcase and shook it against his ear — opened it. The contents were uninteresting. A batch of company minutes. A few confidential directives. The secretary's name figured on each document. He put the briefcase back in place and went into the bedroom.

The front of the built-in closet slid back on rollers. His nose caught the intimate scent of a woman's clothing. He held the pencil-flash between his teeth, leaving both hands free. He felt past the dresses till he found heavier stuff. He played the light on the suits.

A charcoal gray jacket was shiny at the elbows. He lifted out the hanger and carried it across to the bed. He sat down, heart hammering, sure now that he'd found what he'd come for.

He placed the flashlight on the bed beside him so that its beam slanted across his lap. He felt in the inside pocket of the jacket. Three keys were in a small leather wallet. He drew them out on a ring. The business end of each key was finely machined. The smallest had two sets of wards, one opposed to the other. He pulled a small cigar box from his trenchcoat pocket. The front had been cut away. Resting in a bed of cotton were three pieces of cuttlefish bone — white as chalk but tougher, more granulated. The surfaces of each piece had been scraped flat. He held the first key laterally, and sank it into the cuttlefish bone. He reversed the key and made a second impression — poked the end of the shank into the friable material. The impressions were sharp and definitive. He repeated the maneuver with the other two keys and packed the cigar box with cotton which he took out of a plastic bag. He used more cotton to pad the exterior and put the box in the bag.

He weighed it experimentally in his hand. Another page from the Burglar's Manual. He put the keys back in the inside pocket of the jacket and replaced the hanger in the closet. He checked the carpet where he'd been sitting — the bed — straightened the coverlet. The clock was chiming eight as he crossed the hall into the sitting room. He pulled back the curtain. A high wind carried the pelting rain slantways across the face of the building. A dark wash of water blurred the forecourt ten stories below. Thorne's station wagon was parked directly underneath. Cameron flashed a signal. The headlamps responded immediately, lighting the forecourt for the fraction of a second. He lifted the sash. Thorne was standing looking up at him, holding a reversed umbrella. Cameron let the bag go. Thorne moved a yard and trapped it in the upturned umbrella. He was in the car and away before Cameron had time to close the window.

He moved from the curtains. It had been almost *too* easy — the ball bouncing precisely as Henry had said it would. All that was left now was to get out of the place. Even that the Big Brain had taken care of.

Unlock the front door and stash the key in one of the garbage cans on the stairs. If you're challenged, your cover story is perfect. You're looking for Doctor Hewetson. He's in Bermuda? Too bad, you'll have to find another gastroenterologist. A search of your person? Why not — you're a public-spirited citizen. This is all you have — a little cash, a pen and a lighter. A wallet with some snapshots of a blonde. As a matter of fact she happens to be somebody else's wife, but you never heard of a law against it.

He went into the bathroom, spat into the bowl and pulled the flush. He had the key in his hand ready to unlock the front door when he heard someone move outside. A woman's voice called, "Pauline." He cut the flash and backed away. He closed the sitting room door and picked up the phone. He dialed and saw Thorne run from the car to the booth. A click signaled the connection. Cameron's voice sounded as though it hadn't been used in a long while.

"Someone's at the door. A woman. Ringing the bell."

"Go out the kitchen window," Thorne said promptly. "You can reach the roof. Get rid of the skeleton key and don't panic." He hung up.

Cameron tiptoed through the darkened hall. A shadow crossed the strip of light showing at the bottom of the door. He moved away silently, an extra sense guiding him past obstacles in the kitchen. The refrigerator whirred behind him. He stopped dead, a nerve twitching under his left eye, mouth dry.

The window catch was off, the top sash lowered for ventilation. He pulled it down as far as it would go. He spread his handkerchief on the sill, put a foot up and swung himself onto the outside ledge. He reached back for the handkerchief and restored the window to its original position. The ledge he was perched on was set in the leeward side of the building. The rain drove across the deep well, beating on the opposite wall. Lighted windows marked each of the ten stories. He turned his back on them. It was a long way down. Water gurgled in the overhead guttering. He reached up till his fingers touched the metal rim. They hooked onto it like vises. His feet left the ledge and he dangled in the void. The guttering took his weight. He dragged himself up till his chin was level with the flat roof. His forearms were shaking with effort. One last desperate heave, a twist of his body, brought his right knee over the guttering. He rolled away from the edge and staggered to his feet. Wind and rain buffeted his head. His hands were trembling violently, but he was only conscious of one thing — he was safe.

The roof seemed vast. The creaking he heard came from the communal television mast straining against its guy-wires. Far off to the south, headlamps traced the path of the traffic traversing the park. He trotted over to the nearest fire escape. It zigzagged down the face of the inside wall, fifty feet away from the window he'd climbed through. There was no sign of alarm — no hue and cry — no fresh lights. He lowered himself onto the iron stairway and made his way slowly down.

The stretch of wet asphalt at the bottom was a haven of friendly shadows. He dropped the skeleton key down the first drain he came to and ducked through the line of parked cars. As he turned the end of the block, he saw the station wagon cruising towards him. He scrambled in, expecting to hear the shrill of a police whistle. Thorne put his foot down. The car gathered speed. He drove west and north, entering the park near Queen's Road. He stopped under a tree opposite the armory. He lowered the volume of the radio.

"What happened?" he asked casually.

There were wet patches on Cameron's trenchcoat where he'd rolled across the roof. His trouser legs were soaked, the muscles in his forearms stiff and aching. And all this bastard said was, "What happened?" — as though he'd tripped in the middle of a goddam gavotte. He clenched his fist round the lighter and lit a cigarette.

"*Nothing* happened."

Thorne had taken off his overcoat. He tugged at the lapel of his tweed jacket, nodding thoughtfully.

"Someone came to the front door," he prompted. "A woman. What did she do — what did she say?"

Cameron dragged hard on the cigarette. Rain dripped from the overhanging branches, striking the front of the car with metallic regularity. He'd have given a lot to be able to knock this coffin-faced jerk off his perch. It was a while before he trusted himself to answer. He managed somehow to match Thorne's airiness of manner.

"She rang the bell twice and called out 'Pauline.'"

Thorne nibbled the end of his fingernail. "How long was this after you'd gone in? I want to know exactly what you did, Bruce. Try to remember everything. I *have* to know. There's a lot of money hanging on the answer."

Cameron pitched his butt through the open window. He watched rain quench the glow. "A lot of money" was right. And something else that Thorne just might have forgotten. He retraced his steps without committing a detail. It gave him perverse satisfaction to underplay his escape. Thorne's voice was faintly ironical.

"You realize what you did, of course. That woman almost certainly lives in a neighboring flat. She'd probably heard all about the theater tickets. Suddenly the plug's pulled in a bathroom she knows should be empty." His eyes hooded briefly then he smiled.

Cameron felt the flush rising above his collar — as though he'd been caught out in some particularly stupid lie. The idea stretched the tenuous bond between them to breaking point. Caution clamped down on his hostility.

"I never gave it a thought," he admitted.

Thorne switched on the motor. "I'm sure you didn't. The people who don't, usually finish up in stir. As it is we've been lucky. Nothing's missing from the flat. You say you didn't disturb anything. You're absolutely sure that you wiped those keys clean — they couldn't have traces of cuttlefish bone on them?"

Cameron answered with sudden heat. "How many times do you have to hear it — no!"

Thorne fiddled his way into low gear. "Then we've nothing to worry about. The woman will convince herself that she made a mistake. She'll think the noise came from one of the other toilets. I'll call Robin. He can tell his man to get cracking. Where do you want to be dropped — Oakley Street? I'd say let's go and have a drink but Jamie'll be waiting."

Cameron's eyes were steady. Holding a goddam candle, no doubt — with her lips parted and her honey hair catching the light. Only not for long, she'd be waiting. He lifted his hand.

"Sure. Oakley Street's good."

HENRY CADWALLADER THORNE
Wednesday, 22nd December

THE NUMBER continued to ring, a two-note summons that went unanswered. He waited a few more seconds then put the phone down. He cleared the steamed glass with the heel of his glove. Over on the other side of the street a morose figure was hawking wilted chrysanthemums from a pushcart. The lights along King's Road had been burning since early morning. Last minute shoppers undaunted by the bitter cold loitered in the front of the Christmas displays. The coffee bars were crowded with the trendsetters. Unemployed television directors, actors who were "resting" — Chelsea's own brand of model-girl.

He opened the door of the booth, draping the hood of his dufflecoat round his neck, like a scarf. He dragged the brown cap over his eyes and crossed the street. He turned south at the traffic signals, an unobtrusive figure, slightly pigeon-toed. The five-storied houses on each side of the street had long since been converted into flats and bed-sitting rooms, impersonal shelters with an S.W. 3 postal address. Each house had a basement connected to the street by an exterior flight of steps. He stopped after a hundred yards

13

and bent over a shoelace. No one was behind him. He pushed open the iron gate and ran lightly down the steps.

The basement area was ill lit and unsavory. A dead rubber plant drooped in a pot. Rust-colored ice scarred the cracked water pipe. A soiled visiting card was thumbtacked on the entrance door. It was just possible to read the name almost obliterated by penciled messages. *Bruce Cameron.* There was no bellpush. Thorne rapped softly on the knocker. The noise was lost in the sound of the overhead traffic. He pressed his shoulder against the paneling and fed a five-inch strip of mica into the space between the door and the jamb. He lowered the pliable material till it hit the top of the metal cup. Brief manipulation forced back the spring-loaded lock. He stepped inside swiftly and shut the door after him. The dark passage stank of mice. He groped forward, feeling his way along the wall to a door on his right. He turned the handle slowly. The only light in the room came from the window in front of him, ten feet below street level. A few minutes in any neighborhood junk store could have produced the motley collection of furniture. Unmatched armchairs with stained covers. A single divan bed with a yellow corduroy jacket. The floor was covered with jute matting. Travel posters blistered by damp billowed on the whitewashed walls. The three articles on the table were obviously new — a goosenecked reading lamp, a fan heater and a portable typewriter

He went to the table, whistling softly through his teeth. A copy of *Roget's Thesaurus* pinned down a pile of manuscript. The cover was ringed with beer stains, blackened by cigarette burns. He lifted the top page of the manuscript.

To Dissolve a Partnership
by
Bruce Cameron

He read the first few paragraphs, his mouth sardonic. He replaced the book and manuscript and went down the passage to the bedroom. He lifted a corner of the curtain. The window overlooked a patch of ragged grass. The bare plane trees outside were strung with plastic clotheslines. The brick walls enclosing the tiny garden were pitted by weather. He dropped the curtain and switched on the bedside lamp. The bed was unmade. Notebooks and a pencil lay on the floor by its side. A dark blue suit on a hanger dangled from the handle of the clothes closet. He circled the bed and stood in front of the dressing-table mirror. A snapshot of a blond girl was tucked into the frame. The pose showed her with head thrown back, laughing, her eyes screwed up tight against the bright sunshine. There was an untidy scrawl across the print:

Keep me as happy as this forever, darling! Jamie

His mouth grew thin. He sat on the side of the bed, weighing the three keys in the palm of his hand.

Each was a perfect example of skilled precision work. He tooled them in the machine shop of the Battersea Trades School. The originality of the idea appealed to him. Breaking into an establishment that taught the craft of locksmithing — using its facilities to make false keys to open a strongroom. It was more than original — it was brilliant. Gunn and Cameron knew about one set of keys — but didn't know about these. The second set was his own small surprise. He looked round the bedroom, his mind photographing every detail, then switched off the light. He went through the bathroom into the kitchen. It showed the obvious signs of a man living alone. The refrigerator stacked with empty bottles, packaged soups and quick-serve meals in tinfoil containers. A pot of congealed beans flanked the remains of Cameron's breakfast.

Thorne opened the gas oven, struck a match and turned on a valve. The grease-blocked burners spluttered noisily. Cameron's homecooking didn't appear to involve the use of anything more than a saucepan and griddle. The oven hadn't been used in months. Sheets of enameled metal lined it, leaving a quarter-inch gap between these and the iron frame. He dropped the keys into this space. They rattled to the bottom. He went back to the front room, smiling.

His timing had to be absolutely accurate — Gunn and Cameron must feel relaxed — sure of themselves. What was even more important was that they had to feel sure of him. He sat down at the typewriter, shot his cuffs and hit the keys clumsily with gloved fingers.

YOU WANT THREE MEN FOR THE PALATON JOB!

Henry Thorne, 20 Bywater Mews, S.W.3
Bruce Cameron, 375b Oakley St., S.W.3
Robin Gunn, 66 Holland Court, W.8

He took an envelope from a package on the table and banged out the address in capital letters.

THE COMMISSIONER OF POLICE
NEW SCOTLAND YARD
WHITEHALL, S.W.1

He stamped and gummed the envelope and put it in an inside pocket of his jacket. They'd get it at the Yard first thing in the morning — with his own name at the top of the list. That was surely near genius and not to be spoiled by embellishments — no watertight alibi to provoke suspicion. He'd spend the evening with Jamie. When the police asked him where he'd been, he'd be sure of other places but vague about times. He'd answer their questions with the right combination of shock and indignation — one arm round Jamie, perhaps. *A warrant to search here — my house? You must be joking, officer!* As they started taking the place apart, he could add something about his solicitor or member-of-parliament.

He leaned forward, resting his elbows on top of the typewriter. Cameron was as good as in jail this very minute. The keys hidden in the oven clinched it. The prosecution would prove beyond doubt that they fitted the Palaton strongroom. Gunn's conviction would be even easier. He'd be the only one who showed his face on the job. He'd be put up on an identification parade and he'd be picked out. What they found in his mother's flat would only be make-weight.

He fingered the pile of manuscript thoughtfully. Both men were too sophisticated to panic immediately. The police would go to work on whomever they judged the weaker. He imagined the scene. There'd be the classic team with the tough detective-sergeant, his kindly superior — moving in with a mixture of threat and cajolery designed to shake a suspect's belief in his partner's loyalty. He wondered who'd be first to crack. Probably Robin. Bruce was made of tougher stuff.

He stood up, looking round to make sure that the room was left exactly as he'd found it. In the last analysis, it didn't matter if they both proved heroes. They'd be in and he'd be out. Reliable Henry, making all the right moves for his pals. Providing the cash for their needs in remand prison, a first-class lawyer battling to get them out on bail. With the Palaton payroll still missing, the police would make sure no bail was granted.

He walked as far as the end of the passage and waited there, gauging the sounds that came from outside. Satisfied, he opened the door and ran swiftly up the steps. He cut across King's Road and headed north towards Chelsea Square, his nose muffled in his coat. He turned right behind the fire station, making for his parked car. He loitered in front of the hospital notice board as if reading it. Most thieves learned the lines of a police car the hard way. His own knowledge had come after patient research. He'd sat through long summer days in a hired car left near the main entrance to the Central Police Garage. Slumped behind the wheel, he'd studied every vehicle that went in or out. He made notes of number plates, memorized makes and models. V8 Daimlers, Mark II Jaguars, 3-liter Rovers. The cabs on contract-hire driven by cops in plainclothes. Frosted-food vans, furniture removal vans, the motor scooters the police used in their leap-frog tailing technique. It was a long list, but he'd mastered it. Till he was able to recognize the squad cars sliding through the traffic, crewed by unsmiling men shiftier eyed than their quarry. They congregated outside racetracks, theaters, the stadiums on big fight nights. And he passed through their net like a ghost.

He turned away from the notice board and opened the door of the station wagon. He sat there motionless for a moment, projecting his mind forward to the Old Bailey courtroom. He'd attended enough trials to be able to furnish the atmosphere. It was a production where the cast and stage directions never varied. The wigged and gowned figures sitting at counsel's bench — the judge high on his dais, huddled under a gold and scarlet emblem. Directly below would be the long table where detectives and solici-tors faced one another, opponents in a contest with the liberty of two men at stake. Bruce and Robin would be in the dock, estranged by then and sus-picious of one another. The public gallery would be full, and he'd be somewhere in the middle of the front row, obvious to anyone who cared to look. To the two prisoners he'd represent the last link with free-dom. The police would see him as a man with a nat-ural interest in the outcome of the trial. A respecta-ble stamp dealer, anonymously accused of a crime. They might have doubts about him but he'd be beyond proof of guilt.

He used the gearshift, keeping his eyes on the mir-ror. He drove north along the main thoroughfares till he reached a block angling the south side of Ken-sington High Street. He cut in behind the delivery bay of the department store and parked. The station wagon was partially concealed by a five ton truck. He went into the store by a side entrance, joining the crowds milling through the aisles.

Harassed mothers yanked bawling children away from the toy displays. Tweeded women up from the country, wearing bits of dead birds in their hats, made their purchases from tired temporary help.

The phone booths were on the top floor. He waited his turn to use one, his nose deep in a stamp catalog. He stepped into the empty booth and dialed his own number. It was some time before it answered. The delay neither surprised nor deceived him.

He imagined his wife standing in the mews, fumbling desperately with her key as she heard the phone ringing inside. She'd dash breathless — probably after a rendezvous with Cameron — and pick up the phone, her expression completely guileless.

His voice revealed nothing. "It's me, darling. Were there any calls for me this morning?"

"Nothing," she said. "Where on earth *are* you, Henry?"

He lied from force of habit. "In the City. I had to pick up some stuff. This weather's murder! My ears are just about dropping off. How about you?"

She sidestepped the trap neatly. "I haven't moved out of the house. I've been sitting in front of a roaring fire doing my nails. Are you coming home for lunch, darling?"

"No. You go ahead. I've already eaten. I'll be back about two-thirty, Jamie. Robin and Bruce want to see me about something. I said I'd meet them at the house. Bye-bye."

He cradled the phone and fed another coin into the slot. The smile died. *Darling!* She was a good actress. Even in bed she was a good actress, fitting her lover's face to her husband's body. The lover he was supposed to have rescued her from. The "Cruel Canadian" as she'd once called him, swearing that any feeling she'd ever had for Cameron was dead. But he'd been watching them for months, wearing the mask of gentleness she was supposed to appreciate so much. And he'd missed nothing. Neither the unnatural stiffness when

21

she and Bruce met nor the silence that always followed Cameron's leave-taking.

There wasn't any doubt about her treachery. She'd been deceiving him ever since their wedding. Marriage had meant nothing to her. It was no more than just another relationship to be exploited to the full.

He dialed a Kensington number. It rang without reply as he had expected. Mrs. Gunn was at least predictable. Lunch with one of her friends — her bridge club six afternoons out of seven.

Robin and Bruce had had their uses. The overblown deb's delight with his social contacts still intact. The Canadian, nervy and imaginative. They'd had their uses, that was it. A pair of fools who'd hoped to ride into easy money behind *his* brains and expertise. And they were going to be disappointed. Jamie included. She wouldn't go to jail. She'd just *wish* she'd gone.

He left the store by a front exit and weaved his way through the traffic to the north side of Kensington High Street. He skirted the front of the block of flats and walked round to the rear of the building. An alley offered access to the back entrances. He passed loaded trucks, unnoticed by men sheltering from the cold. He turned sharp left into a narrow passage. Straight ahead was the service door leading into the apartment building. It gave under the pressure of his hand. He stepped into a bare concrete hallway. Flicking elevator signals showed the cage to be on its way down.

He ran up the stone stairway. Each landing had a pass door leading to the flats. He climbed to the sixth floor and stepped into the corridor, the key ready in his hand. There were bowls of freesias on a stand, their scent mingling with the smell of floor polish and Virginian cigarettes.

He tiptoed past a dog's bark, the blare of a radio, clattering plates. 66 was the last apartment on the left. He lifted the mail flap and bent down. He heard nothing inside.

He fitted a dropped-E key into the mortise lock. It threw the tumbler at the first attempt. He shut the door, thankful that the second lock hadn't been used. He left his shoes in the hall and padded into the drawing room. The yellow carpet was soft underfoot. The furnishings were roughly what he had expected. A Chippendale table and chairs, a few pieces of old silver, a glass cabinet with oriental figures. Fans, tortoiseshell boxes, some procelain statuettes. An oil painting on the end wall depicted an irritable-looking man dressed in the uniform of the Brigade of Guards. A sprig of holly was attached to the frame. He read the note propped on the mantel. It was written on a slip of paper torn from a bridge pad.

Robin
A girl called "Midge"? telephoned — something about a handbag left somewhere. If you're late to-night please come in quietly.

Mother

He pushed the bedroom door open. The French bed had a velvet padded headboard. Mrs. Gunn's formidable features were framed in a square of silver on the small table. She had the same dark coloring as her son, the same arrogant nose. Bottles of scent and skin conditioners, lipsticks and handcreams suggested a matron still concerned with her appearance. The two bedrooms were connected by a bathroom. The tub was pink with matching tiles and an elaborate makeup table. He grinned, seeing the coronets embroidered on the corners of the towels. But naturally — the *Honorable* Mrs. Gunn — granddaughter of a potbellied Shropshire builder ennobled for party services. The title still existed — but not the money.

He went into Gunn's bedroom warily — as if he expected the tartan rug to be thrown back suddenly, revealing Robin sitting there smiling welcome. The doors of the built-in wardrobe were open. A number of suits and overcoats hung on shaped hangers. Underneath was an array of handmade shoes. His nose thinned. An outfit for every occasion, of course. Ah well, Robin would look less elegant in gray battledress. He felt in his inside pocket, pulled out a large-scale map. An arrowed route had been drawn across it in Chinese ink. The route led from a square marked LODGE GATE to another identified as STRONG-ROOM BUILDING. A reminder was written on the edge of the map. *Check distance from gate to strongroom.*

Thorne folded the map neatly and went down on his knees. He crawled under Gunn's bed. The carpet was tacked to the floor. He pulled an edge free and stuffed the map under the carpet. He crawled out and stood up. The police would have no difficulty proving whose handwriting it was. Like everything else about him, Robin's mark was flamboyant and unmistakable. He found his shoes and waited behind the door till he was sure the corridor was deserted. It was ten minutes past two as he drove off, still smiling.

BRUCE CAMERON
22nd December

HAIL SWEPT the length of the mews. Pellets of ice gathered in the crevices between the cobblestones, rattled against the windows. The flower basket hanging outside the corner house creaked in the wind. The windows on the right of the street door were sealed by drawn curtains. Inside, the three men leaned forward expectantly. Thorne threw a switch on the 8 mm. projector. He took his time, fussing with the focus adjustment till the image was sharp. The film started to unwind. The only sounds in the room were the hum of the motor and the tinny bombardment of hail on the windows.

Cameron narrowed his nostrils. The French cigarettes Robin affected made the place stink like a third-rate bistro. The picture on the wall danced unsteadily, obviously shot from a moving vehicle. A forest of television aerials showed against a sullen sky. A succession of turnpike-Tudor villas was followed by a high brick wall crowned with barbed wire. The wall dropped to a gatehouse guarding a hardtop driveway. The camera panned suddenly, offering a jerky glimpse of factory buildings beyond formidable iron gates. Signs clustered about the entrance.

PALATON — the best in plastics!
SPEED LIMIT FIFTEEN MILES AN HOUR
No admittance except on business

A sprocket clattered and the film broke.

A naked beam of light drove on the white painted wall. It was momentarily blinding. Cameron turned his head away, blinking. Gunn was lolling in his chair, his shoulder blades where his buttocks should have been. A curl of gray smoke hung over his head. He winked at Cameron, a bang of black hair nodding. Cameron stared back impassively, familiar with the rôle Robin was playing. Bonnie Prince Charlie on the eve of battle.

Thorne worked on the projector. The room darkened again. The picture was steady now, giving a head-on view of gates and a driveway framed in a foreground of trees. An armored truck loomed across the lens, pulled off the highway and stopped in front of the gates. A head came out of the nearside door of the cab. A man wearing the uniform of a security corps jumped down. He was back within seconds. He looked up and down the highway as the gatekeeper unfastened the heavy bolts. The guard hoisted himself back in the cab. The truck was driven up the slope and vanished behind a building five hundred yards away. The camera held on the empty driveway. After a while the truck reappeared, blinking its headlamps in the twilight. The gatekeeper hurried out. This time it was the driver who leaned from his window, peaked cap on the back of his head. The truck rolled towards the camera and disappeared again.

Thorne touched a switch behind him. Yellow-shaded candles glowed on the walls. He lowered himself into a chair as if doubtful of its solidity. He sat for a while, silent — twisting the signet ring on his little finger. He was wearing a brown tweed jacket patched with leather on the elbows, a checked flannel shirt and cavalry-twill trousers. A shred of blood-stained paper stuck to his cheekbone at the edge of the razor line.

He pushed his fingers through sparse sandy hair, smiling at Gunn.

"You ought to get an Oscar, Robin. Very professional. One thing bothers me — where were you when you took those last shots?"

Cameron groaned soundlessly. This might well turn into one of Thorne's interminable interrogations. He always justified them by referring to his lack of a police record. *I've been a thief for ten years,* etc. Then the piece about paying attention to detail.

Gunn stretched out his arms, a bored and polished performer playing to a houseful of yokels.

"Where *was* I, Henry? I'd say fifteen yards from the main road lying on my face with mud halfway up my nose. Bruce was covering me from behind. While we're on the subject, that clump of trees is as big as a football field. And nobody saw us go in — nobody saw us come out."

Cameron flipped his lighter. He leaned a cigarette into the gas flame and inhaled deeply. He lifted his head, looking directly at Thorne.

"That's right. We left the car half a mile away. Nobody saw us because there wasn't anyone there."

Thorne cranked himself up, leaned his shoulder against the edge of the mantelpiece and scratched vigorously, continuing to smile.

"First class. You know what they say — the unconsidered detail that spells the difference between success and disaster."

Gunn bent his head sideways till his nose touched the cornflower in his lapel. He clamped his hands together lightly, eyes flicking a derisive signal at Cameron.

"And we live in parlous times," he said.

Screened radiators wafted gusts of hot air. The room was too warm for comfort. Cameron hung his jacket over the back of his chair. Above the mantelpiece was a large Dufy print — an impression of sun, jockeys and thoroughbred horses. The books piled on the three-tiered shelves reflected Thorne's varied interests. *The Meaning of Reason,* Keylock's *Dams of Winners, The Report of the Commissioner of Metropolitan Police,* 1964–65, some tomes dealing with philately. Cameron dribbled smoke from his mouth.

"We missed nothing, Henry. They trucked the payroll in at precisely four-thirty-seven. Seager managed to get a look at the check stub in the secretary's office. Sixty-one thousand, one hundred and forty-seven pounds. A week's pay for twelve hundred men plus their Christmas bonus and club benefit. The money's being stored overnight in the strongroom. It'll stay there until nine o'clock tomorrow morning. Then the pay clerks start processing it. There's no way of telling whether or not the bills are in series. Sometimes they are, sometimes they're not, according to Seager. I'd say we have to reckon on some of the bills being new. But we always figured that to be a possibility."

Gunn's stub was smoldering on the table beside him. Thorne ground it out, his mouth fastidious. A door slammed somewhere upstairs. He cocked his head like a ginger-polled bird. Footsteps descended. He put his fingers on the freckles spreading across his nose as if he could feel them.

"What about Seager, Robin — he's your production. Are we going to trust his accuracy a hundred percent? It's always been my experience that people like that — peddlers of information — are incapable of being truthful or accurate. There's too much wishful thinking going on — a tendency to forget detail. You know the sort of thing — the friend of the owner of the flat you're burgling — the one who comes in to feed the goldfish halfway through the performance." He made a circle in the air and punched a hole in it.

Gunn moved even lower on his shoulder blades. He drew the tips of his shoes together as if the maneuver were of supreme importance. But he said nothing. Cameron answered for him.

"Why do you always have to put on this Cassandra

act? Seager's a scientist. Scientists have a bias towards accuracy. Everything he's told us up to now has turned out correct. You've been inside the strongroom. He described every inch of it for you — the location of the burglar alarm — everything. So what the hell's worrying you — the sixty-one thousand? I was in the bank when they drew the money. I don't claim to be able to count at a distance of twenty feet — anyway I had other things to think about. But three sacks went out on the trolley. Three *large* sacks."

Thorne crossed the room swiftly and turned the key in the door leading to the hall. Gunn moved the top half of his body, his smile insolent.

"You give me the creeps, Henry. What did you expect — an affidavit from the bank manager?"

Thorne's neck flushed. "I'll tell you what I expect — an understanding of what I'm trying to do — keep us out of jail. Let me remind you exactly how much you've contributed to this venture up to date. A chance meeting with Seager — a man you happened to be at school with — an hour or so with a cine-camera. Bruce has done more than his share. But *I'm* the one who turned your joint efforts into a practical proposition. And unless you're willing to continue on that basis, I'm quite ready to pull out."

Cameron's eyebrows bent. Without Thorne's expertise, the keys were useless. Everyone in the room knew it. He tried to stop the younger man before more damage was done.

"Why don't you belt up! We know you're the hottest thing since Raffles, but in this case Henry's right."

Gunn spread his hands. His good-looking features were unrepentant.

"Henry's *always* right. That's why I love him."

Thorne's smile made ironic acknowledgment. "Thank you, Robin. Perhaps you'd like to offer an informed opinion about what I'm going to say. A Hungarian refugee called Jeraczi started Palaton Plastics. He still owns seventy-five percent of the shares. People like the Jeraczis have been hiding their money for generations. You know the form — from the Cossacks down to the Commissars. That sort of thing leaves a mark. No wonder the security arrangements he makes are tight. But what happens next according to Seager? They lock the money up and walk away, whistling. It's left unguarded for two whole nights and a day. *You* accept that without comment, both of you — it disturbs me."

Gunn unwound his legs. "I'm waiting for the day when you're *unable* to discover something that disturbs you, 'without comment!' What are we supposed to say? The Palaton payroll's only as big as this once a year. They've never been robbed. They're leaving the money in a building specially designed to keep out people like us — with a burglar alarm connected directly to the police station. 'Left unguarded!' — Balls!"

Cameron sneaked a look at Thorne. His feeling was that they were both being tested — being forced to reason. The trouble was that Robin always found it hard to take.

"Let's drop it, for Crissakes," he said. "You're exaggerating, Henry. I've checked out every piece of information that hasn't come from Seager. It's Christmas week. That means they're only working one shift at the factory — eight to five. By a quarter-past, the only people left in the joint are the night staff — a couple of maintenance men in the powerhouse and the gatekeeper. There's one old guy who patrols Administration and Research. Nobody goes near the strongroom. You've been in there yourself. How many watchmen did *you* see?"

Thorne rubbed his neck slowly. "None. But that was at eleven o'clock on a Sunday morning when the strongroom was empty. There's over sixty-one thousand pounds in it at this moment."

Cameron dragged at the knot in his tie. "Your thoughts are profound. But it so happens I'm going into the strongroom with you. I'm as worried about my hide as you are."

Gunn reached out, still yawning and stretching. "We *both* are, Henry. You know me — the dedicated follower of fashion. And I'll be showing my face— all you've got to do is open the strongroom."

Thorne explored his pockets. He came up with a well-used pipe and sucked on it emptily.

"You've got a positive talent for oversimplication."

Cameron was suddenly sick of it all. Thorne's caution irritated, but at the same time it gave him confidence. It had been like that ever since the first night he'd followed Thorne up a stranger's stairway — a criminal from the moment that the key had been turned in the lock. He'd stood in the darkened room, listening with his stomach to the breathing of the woman sleeping in the four-poster bed. Thorne's indifference to danger had reassured him. His own had gradually become second nature. The feeling of confidence was still there, reluctant tribute to the man he secretly hated.

"Why don't we run the other film?" he asked. "We're either going to hit this place or we're not."

Thorne smiled. "I think there's merit in the suggestion." He fitted another spool into the projector and cut the lights. The scene he threw on the wall was the same as before. But it was later in the day. The lighted windows of the gate lodge showed through the murk. A white truck crossed in front of the camera and stopped. Painted on its side was the legend AJAX LAUNDRY SERVICE. The truck rolled through the open gates and was lost to sight. They continued to watch in silence though there was no longer movement on the wall. The wire basket outside banged in the wind. The truck reappeared, turned east and headed in the direction of London. Thorne snapped on the wall lights. He looked at his stopwatch.

"Fifteen minutes, eleven seconds — from the time the van went in. We'll allow ourselves ten. It should be more than enough."

Cameron rapped a cigarette on his thumbnail. "I can tell you this much — they haven't changed their routine in a month. The truck shows up some time between half-past five and six. It delivers three hampers of towels and collects the dirty ones."

Thorne crossed the room and pulled the curtain back. The hail still rode on the blustering wind. He turned round.

"The weather is in our favor. We won't have any of those old ladies walking their dogs — old bags looking for somebody else's business to mind. None of those kids with an itch to jot down license numbers."

"Amen," said Cameron. He pitched his butt at the fireplace. It landed in the brass fender and smoldered. He walked over and put his heel on it. He was taller than either of the others. His hair appeared to have been trimmed with a pair of garden shears. The lines from nose to mouth were deep — as if he smiled or snarled with equal readiness. His blue eyes were almost without expression — as though communication between them and the rest of his face had snapped. He turned his stare on Thorne.

"I took the van over to the warehouse this morning. It's the same make, year and color as the real thing. Robin bought it in the name of the Ajax Laundry Service and paid cash. There's a full tank and I put in a new battery. The sign's on the side. Nothing's been forgotten."

Thorne unlocked the door. He stuck his head out into the hall and called. A woman's voice answered. He shut the door again and stood in front of the fireplace sucking his empty pipe.

"The big one at last," he said suddenly. "The one we've made sacrifices for."

Gunn rose. Cupping his hand he blew a mock trumpet call and then scowled.

"The big one at last," he repeated. "What a schmaltzy sod you are some of the time. Don't tell me we're not having prayers."

Thorne continued imperturbably. "We drive straight from the factory to the warehouse and transfer. Then Robin takes the van to the sandpits. Make sure you've enough petrol, Robin. There's got to be a complete burn-out. Then you come back in my car and we make our respective ways home. Any questions?"

Gunn had crossed to the window. He stood there watching the hail bombard the cobblestones. He answered without turning his head.

"I had a word with Seager last night. The laundry van stops two miles up the road — the last stop but one before going to Palaton's. It's a furniture factory with a canteen. The driver always nips in for a cup of tea. Seager's going to leave Research about four. He can do that without anyone asking questions. He'll be waiting outside the canteen. While the driver's inside, Seager will attend to the van."

Thorne's lower lip jutted. "Suppose the driver has a bellyache — suppose he just doesn't *feel* like tea?"

Gunn swung round. His face was resigned — like that of a man asked to tell a story for the tenth time.

"I can't keep anything secret," he said, sarcastically. "The driver's been doing the same thing for the past six weeks — going in for a cup of tea before delivering his laundry. Even if he *doesn't* he still has to leave the van for ten minutes and push a trolley fifty yards and back. Seager will be on his tail. He won't do anything to the van that will alarm — only delay. We thought of unscrewing a fuel pipe. Seager's going to wait in his car outside on the London Road. He'll give us the OK signal as we go by."

A pedestal clock with a brass face shuddered before chiming three times. The door of the hall opened. The girl carrying the tray had fine blond hair sweeping up from a low right-hand parting. A gold buckle near her left cheekbone held it in place. Her long legs were molded in stretch slacks, her breasts high under a cashmere sweater. She walked over in stained ballet shoes to the table that Thorne cleared for her. Her sleeves were pulled up well above her elbows. She lifted the tarnished Georgian teapot, a bracelet sliding down her forearm. She spoke to Thorne in a low voice.

"You didn't say whether you wanted anything to eat. There's lemon if anyone wants it."

Thorne took the pot from her. He smiled as their fingers touched.

"I'll cope, darling."

Her only makeup was a series of bold slashes drawn on silvered lids. The artifice lifted the corners of her dark blue eyes. She met Gunn's easy grin and salute stonily. Cameron framed a greeting. But his lips had suddenly gone dry. Old pain and longing knifed into his stomach. She hesitated for a moment as if she was uncertain what was expected of her.

"Hello, Bruce," she said, then turned and walked

away. She left the room looking straight in front of her.

Gunn balanced his cup and saucer on his knee. The remark he aimed was for anyone who cared to listen. "I'll say this for Jamie—her manners are perfect. I've never known anyone who made me feel more at home."

Thorne's face was withdrawn. "It's possible she doesn't like you, Robin? Some people don't."

Gunn put a hand on his silk shirt, somewhere near his heart. "Just one word, Henry — nonsense! *I'm everyone's* friend. Don't I always treat your wife with homage and respect? You know what it is — somebody must be gossiping about me. What do you think, Bruce? You know her better than I do."

Thorne's cup clattered on the tea tray. "Let's drop the subject, shall we," he said stiffly.

He opened a chest against the wall and dragged out bundles of clothing. He tossed one at each man. Cameron picked up his. The black tracksuit was zippered at the front, gathered at wrists and ankles. All identifying marks had been removed. Even the inner soles had been ripped out of the canvas shoes, the stenciled code marks burned out of the fabric. A pair of wash-leather gloves completed each outfit. Cameron rolled shoes and gloves in the tracksuit. He propped the bundle on his knee and caught the carrier bag Thorne threw him.

"Don't forget," said Thorne. "Nothing in your pockets except enough cash to get home in an emergency. Otherwise nothing — are we all understood?"

Cameron nodded. Thorne started to pace about nervously. He punctuated his remarks with throw-away movements of the hands.

"The law of average — that's the only law I respect. I don't know if it occurs to either of you that all we know about the inside of a prison is what we've read or been told. That's as it should be. But the odds against us acquiring firsthand information increase every time we risk our liberty. I'm making this my last job. If you've got any sense you'll make it yours too."

Cameron hid his contempt. This was the old distilled logic — dropped on the foreheads of less percipient fellows and highly suspect. The way everything connected with Henry was suspect. The phoney apostle of friendship — the thin-lipped ascetic with his hand up the nearest woman's skirt. The bit about violence would come next. And that too was phoney. Thorne had no moral objection to the use of force. All he was worried about was having to use it himself.

Cameron shrugged. "Nobody ever heard me say I enjoyed being a thief — maybe it's what you call my 'built-in Presbyterian conscience,' Henry. All I want to do is to haul my arse into the sun. With twenty thousand quid I can afford to wait till someone wises up to the fact that I can write."

Thorne hooked his heels over the fender. "That's one thing there's no question about, Bruce. And you'll sell because you have talent."

Cameron inclined his head gravely. The judge of genius had spoken — the old talker into the night.

"Great. You encourage me to continue."

Thorne's gesture warned off the Canadian's irony. "What about you, Robin?"

Gunn stretched one more time like an old hound in hot sunshine.

"I keep getting hold of these books — you know the sort of thing — *I Was a Teenage Counterfeiter!* With a dedication to 'Shirl — the girl who waited.' The details are always disgusting. Porridge, mailbag — sewing — homemade knives and romances with someone called 'Big Charlie.' It's not my form, really."

Thorne picked the shred of a paper from his cheekbone. He glanced at the fresh flow of blood with surprise before stanching it with his handkerchief.

"I wouldn't have thought so. Anyway. What I really wanted to say was that I appreciate the way you've both accepted my decisions. More money was stolen by violence last year than by all other methods put together. But that's only half the story, isn't it?"

Gunn moved back to the window. He followed a trickle of water down the outside of the pane with his forefinger.

"It is indeed. Not only are our hearts pure — we stayed clear of the constabulary."

Thorne dabbed at his cheek with his handkerchief. He seemed to be paying no more attention to Gunn's sarcasm.

"I've always been against unnecessary risk. I've turned jobs down with one thing in mind — our joint safety. I've seen you both go home, needing money and resentful. Telling yourselves it was all right for me — I could always sell a couple of my bloody stamps and raise a few quid. As it happens, you were right. It must have been difficult to accept — especially for you, Bruce."

Cameron shifted the weight from one leg to another. "Why especially for me?" he said suspiciously.

Thorne's voice was mild. "Because you're violent by nature and a moralist. It's an explosive mixture."

Cameron stared back unblinkingly. "I've mellowed," he said shortly.

Gunn clapped his hands together. "Listen to me, children — before you're both entirely carried away by this deeply philosophical conversation. There's one thing I care more about than your exchanges — money. I want the shareout to be tonight. With an equal division and each man free to do what he wants with his share. As far as I'm concerned I intend leaving the country this week."

Thorne looked shocked. "If you're serious, Robin, nobody can stop you leaving the country. But you *can* be stopped from putting Bruce and me in danger."

"Can I?" said Gunn. "How and why?"

The other two men moved uncomfortably in the silence that followed. Thorne's voice was coaxing.

"You agreed to our plan — there's never been any question of it before. I made the arrangements for the cash to be transferred out of the country. You each draw your share at the end of six months — wherever you like, in whatever currency you like. The same way that I did. Seager gets five percent — there's another ten percent for the handling. It still leaves seventeen thousand apiece. Why have you suddenly changed your mind?"

Gunn shrugged. "I'm a worrier. I keep asking myself — what happens if Henry has an accident?" He smiled but not with his eyes. "Or something."

Thorne was patient. "You get your share with whatever interest has accrued. The money's held in equal amounts, three accounts. What do you think you both gave me signatures for. Are you in this too, Bruce?"

Cameron stared back. If Thorne wanted a Scotch he went to the drinks cupboard. Robin had keys to a couple of apartments where he didn't have to pay the rent. Both were a long way from a basement flat stinking of other people's garbage. He threw his support to Thorne because he had to.

"I'm not in it, no. He gets his money when we do. And come to think of it I wouldn't want to be around then."

Gunn shook his head slowly. "What's the matter, Bruce, don't you like me either?"

Cameron widened his stare. "Why not — I've got nothing else to do."

Thorne cut in hastily. "For God's sake, let's stop this bickering. We're grown men. I wanted to tell you this if you'd given me a chance. Neither of you'll go short of money while you're waiting. I'm willing to pay you a hundred pounds each every month, deducted from your share. And just so there's no confusion, it'll be *my* money you're spending — earned and taxed. We're not thugs — we're gentlemen and comrades."

Cameron made no pretense of hiding his smile. There it went again — the same old flag. Thorne ran it up the pole and everyone was supposed to stand to attention and salute. The truth was the Fate Sisters had brought them together. And the only thing that bound them was expediency.

"I think I'll go get a glass of water," he said suddenly.

Gunn ducked his head, apparently concerned with his nails. He looked over at the desk. The cut-glass jug next to the whiskey bottle was full of water.

"Of course, Bruce. You know where to get it."

Cameron closed the door quietly behind him. He stood for a moment in the hall, glancing up the stairs. Coats, a pajama jacket, a swirl of chiffon scarves, dangled from the banisters. Some fishing rods were propped in a corner of the hall. Hanging on a hook above them was the dirty dufflecoat Thorne wore like a goddam cloak of invisibility. Creeping about in it, cracking his knuckles. Henry Cadwallader Thorne, gentleman at crime and comrade at arms.

He turned the handle of the kitchen door. Jamie was leaning against the open refrigerator, almost as if she had been waiting for him. He took a deep breath, going back in time. The scene was the basement flat on Oakley Street all over again. The same dirty dishes in the sink — the same vegetables sprouting in a mildewed basket. And stacked in the fridge would be the familiar remains of meals long since forgotten. All the old confusion and profligacy that was Jamie's trademark.

He leaned back, pushing his shoulders against the door. The cat perched on the window sill started to growl softly, its tail featherdusting the wall. He wet his lips with the tip of his tongue.

"He won't come in while I'm here, Jamie. I just wanted you to know that it's come at last. The chance I've been waiting for. In a few months there'll be enough dough to buy a patch of sunshine for us both. We're going to put this year behind us, Jamie, and going back where we started. We'll be the way we always used to be — together."

She cocked her head. The red-shaded light tinged her blond hair the color of a robin's breast. Her voice was scarcely audible.

"What are you going to do?"

He moved his head impatiently. "What do you care what I'm going to do! Listen to me — this is our last chance — we can't afford to louse it up. There's too much at stake. We can make things better than ever they were. This bit with Thorne — who the hell gives a damn! Divorce him or don't divorce him — you don't love him. You never loved him, Jamie."

She nudged the refrigerator door with her knee. Her eyes searched the room as though looking for an excuse to postpone her answer. She came across to the table very slowly, sat down and cleared a space. She put her head between her hands. It was some time before she replied. Her voice had the desperate de-

44

termination of a mother attempting reason with an obstinate child.

"*Can't* you understand or is it that you *won't*, Bruce? It's all over. It was over and done with a year ago. People's feelings change. You told me that yourself once, remember?"

He had no thirst but he poured himself a glass of water and drank it. He pushed his hands deep in the pockets of his jacket so that she would not see that they were shaking. "That was something else and you know it. I was hurt — jealous — but not serious."

She peeped through her hands, her voice sad. "You were never more serious in your life."

He denied the accusation vehemently. "You must be crazy! What sort of guy do you think I am! What did you expect me to say — that what happened between you and Thorne was bound to happen? That I was as much to blame as you were? OK. I'll say it now — I was as much to blame as you were. Did that justify this tasteless joke of a marriage? You know it as well as I do — we'll go on loving one another till the sun drops out of the sky."

She shook her head, her hands buried in her hair. "Don't, Bruce! Please don't! It's doing neither of us any good. What we both need is emotional sanity — can't you see that?"

He battered at the chink he thought he saw. "Look, be fair, Jamie. I was working fourteen hours a day, putting words on paper that nobody wanted to buy. Eating in a stinking basement on your money. Don't

45

you see how that can warp a man's mind? For Chrissakes, I'd reached the point where I was blaming *you* for the squalor we lived in. A man just isn't normal living like that."

He cut himself short rather than complete the memory. It still pumped blood into his brain. The flat crowded with the dispossessed of Chelsea — cheap bums flying on cheap wine, playing at rebellion. At that time Thorne hadn't been anything more than an undefined visitor from a world of plenty — a seeker of the swinging scene, who arrived with a bottle of Teacher's Highland Cream, wearing an odor of eau de Portugal and offering the women understanding. Sly, erudite Henry, the patron of the arts. Loud above the boozy hubbub, he remembered his own voice as he tried to put Jamie down — to belittle whatever she might say. Resentful of other people's interest in her. As if some maniacal need drove him to assert his superiority.

She took her hands away from her face. What looked like compassion showed in her deep blue eyes.

"I'm sorry for you — desperately sorry. You're still the same old Bruce, demanding recognition on any terms that you choose to make. I loved you more than I ever hope to love again. I don't think I'd want to — not in the same violent, consuming way. Now that's over. You could have stopped it — you could have kept the love alive. God knows it would have been easy. A little pity and understanding — that's all it would have taken. But you had to punish me instead.

A woman can only take so much punishment — guilty or not."

He rinsed his glass mechanically and poured himself a second shot of water. Anger tempted him to the major denunciation. He didn't know how many times she had slept with Thorne nor where nor when it had started. He didn't want to know.

The first shocked realization of her treachery still unnerved him. They'd been sitting in the basement flat, facing one another in the twilight. He'd broken the silence with savage accusal, taking her throat in his hands, choking the very admissions he was shouting for. He'd let her go, shaking with rage and frustration. Despair followed. Despair and a stubborn refusal to believe that this could be happening to *him*. Days passed. Verbal lashings followed the physical violence till he was no longer making sense not even to himself.

He tried to put it all out of his mind. "That's a lot of crap, Jamie. I know you better than you know yourself. I still may have to wait but you'll come in the end."

It was as if she were trying to recall something half-forgotten.

"Why *won't* you understand, Bruce? It's too late. I offered to go away with you once, remember just after it had happened. We'd gone for a walk in St. James's Park. I can remember the ducks — an old lady feeding them who kept watching us. I told you the truth then — I'd have gone anywhere with you and been faithful till the end of time. You refused because you still wanted to punish me. That's when I gave up, Bruce. Something shriveled inside me."

He walked across the room to her. He stood looking at her for a while and then kissed her, forcing his mouth through her closed lips. She stayed quite still, her eyes shut, till he released her.

He tried one last time. "Jamie!"

She opened her eyes. The look in them shattered his pride. Another woman's voice sounded in his brain. The voice of a stranger at a bar, clipped and contemptuous — ". . . then he begged me to take him back, my dear. Can you imagine, a man *begging!*"

She jumped up, speaking very quietly. "Please let me alone."

The cat streaked for shelter as his voice toughened. He tried for words that would wound her.

"You dirty whore!"

She backed away as far as she could. Her expression was frightened but her eyes were resolute.

"Is that what you call every woman who's done what I've done?"

He stopped inches from her. There was a scar visible over her right eyebrow. A scar he was responsible for.

"For God's sake, Jamie," he said. "Is this the way it's all going to end — hating one another?"

Strain showed in her face. "I don't hate anybody — you least of all. You're right about Henry. I don't love anyone either. But he's given me things I never had before. Gentleness and understanding. For those I'm grateful."

He went on, unable to stop himself. "The sweetest story ever told. What the hell sort of basis is that for a life together — gentleness and understanding! I can give you everything he has and more. And this time there'll be no money worries. I need you, Jamie. Doesn't that *mean* anything?"

The expression in her eyes softened. "A great deal. You may not think so, but I worry about you. I've known for months that there's something going on between you, Henry and Robin. I don't ask questions — I never have. But I'm sure of one thing. Robin's bad for you both. Why don't you get out of London, Bruce? Out of England. Go home!"

"Home?" he repeated incredulously. Ghosts grimaced from the past, making a mockery of the word.

She persisted obstinately. "That's right — home. If not to your family at least to Canada."

He stepped back, shaking his head. "What are you trying to do to me, Jamie?"

She stood, her hands pressing against the wall behind her. She answered, looking him full in the face. "Help you."

He turned away abruptly and wrenched the kitchen door open. Back in the sitting room, Thorne was reading a newspaper ostentatiously. Gunn's smile was knowing. Cameron looked at him. "What's on *your* mind?"

Gunn shrugged. "I was thinking it's getting late."

Cameron's mouth snarled. "Then why not get your arse out of that chair!"

Thorne saw them into the hall. He helped Cam-

eron with the smart raincoat, his foxy face expression-
less. He inched the door back and looked up the
mews. The hail had changed to snow blown by a fitful
northeaster. He jerked his head at them. "OK — I'll
say goodbye to Jamie for you."

His eyes held Cameron's for the fraction of a second. Then he smiled. Cameron nodded. The hell
with him. And if Jamie wanted to open her mouth,
the hell with him again.

"Do that," he said shortly. "Half-past five."

He bent his head into the weather, holding his hat
on with both hands. He had a strong feeling of having done it all before. And then he remembered.

It had snowed the day Jamie left him. He'd returned home crocked to find her gone — the flat
stripped of her possessions. Everything he had ever
given her had been left on the sitting room table. The
topaz ring and sheepskin jacket — the watch he had
bought with the money that came from his first published story. There was no letter — no indication
where she had gone. He'd sat in the dark, listening to
the footsteps on the sidewalk overhead. Fifty times
he told himself that she'd be back. That she'd done
this to teach him a lesson. In a little while he'd hear
the gate creak open. Then she'd run down the steps
and rattle the flap on the mailbox. She'd come into
the room, looking at him as she sometimes did, frown-
ing and smiling at the same time.

"You're silly," she'd say.

He'd take her in his arms and the misery of the last
weeks would be forgotten. But he didn't.

It was after ten before he could bring himself to accept the truth. She'd left and she wasn't coming back. He got up very slowly, moving round the flat in the darkness. He hadn't wanted to see himself in the mirror. The gun was hidden in the bottom of his clothes closet, souvenir of a trip to Tangier. The mere fact of having it had always given him a feeling of security. If ever the time came to use it, there'd at least be no anticlimax. No drowsy doctor using a pump on a bellyful of barbiturates. Just one quick jerk on the trigger and oblivion.

He took the thirty-eight caliber automatic from its oilskin bag, checked the clip and moved a shell into the breach. He put the gun in his overcoat pocket and climbed the steps to the street. The snow had been an inch thick by the time he reached Bywater Mews. Everything there was clean, silent and sparkling. He padded over to the corner house, put his thumb on the door buzzer and pressed. Television was loud inside. He pressed the buzzer again and hit the door with the heel of his hand. The door opened suddenly. A shaft of light from the hall knifed into the mews. Thorne was wearing a camel's hair robe over his pajamas. He removed the pipe from his mouth, standing aside to let Cameron come in. He opened the sitting room door, still saying nothing. He stood like an actor waiting for his cue. Melting snow dripped from Cameron's shoes onto the light blue carpet. He looked directly into Thorne's face.

"Make it easy on yourself — where is she?"

He remembered a stamp catalog on the table —

some small cellophane envelopes. Thorne had started putting them into a briefcase, one after another very slowly. He placed the briefcase on top of the bookshelf and carried a couple of glasses to the table. He poured two fingers of Scotch into a tumbler and pushed it in Cameron's direction. Then he poured himself a drink. The gun in Cameron's hand seemed to fascinate him.

"I don't know," he answered.

The Scotch fired Cameron's stomach. "Maybe this'll help your memory." He raised the gun.

Thorne put his glass down as if it were a detonator that would explode the table. "If you want sense from me, put that thing away. I can't talk with it pointing at me."

Cameron sighted along the barrel. "I ought to blow your head off."

Thorne's cheeks had gone the color of cheese. "That's nonsense and you know it. They'd have you before the night was out."

Cameron grinned. The whiskey was getting its work in. "That wouldn't help you"

Thorne moved very slowly, his eyes watchful as he refilled Cameron's glass.

"Put the gun away," he pleaded.

Cameron's glare wavered. He stuck the automatic away, holding onto the butt in his pocket.

"Then talk," he said.

Thorne stood up. He retreated as far as the fireplace. "There's something you've got to understand. Jamie hasn't run away with me — she's run away from

you. If it hadn't been me it would have been someone else, sooner or later. You've got to believe that,
Bruce." He swung round nervously as a coal fell behind him.

Cameron laughed — at Thorne — at himself. An
hour ago he'd have torn Thorne's throat out without
waiting for an explanation. Now all he did was per-
form like an actor in a cheap gangster movie.

"I asked you where she was," he insisted. "You still
haven't answered."

Thorne's thin face was earnest. "I don't know. I
give you my word I don't know. She phoned here just
after seven and told me she was going to a hotel. She
said she'd call me in the morning. I suppose you'd
better know this, we're getting married."

Cameron leaned his head back and laughed. "As a
lesser breed without the law — may I ask if she knows
about this?"

Thorne pulled the cord on his robe. "She knows
about it. We're not going into this blindfolded. I
know that she's still running away from you. It's a
risk all three of us have to take. But we are going to
get married. Short of killing us both there's nothing
you can do to stop it. Why don't you give yourself
enough time to see where *you're* going? Jamie's
out of your life for good — why not start over from
there?"

Cameron's eyes narrowed. "What would *you* suggest?

Thorne gestured briefly. "Writing — it always mattered more to you than she did."

Cameron's fingers tightened on the gun. "Slow down, friend. If you're really what Jamie needs then by God I quit. But keep your nose out of my writing. I'm sensitive." His smile was hard and challenging.

Thorne separated his hands. His voice was persuasive.

"I've read your work and I've seen the way you live. I'm sure that you could be a very good writer. There've been two big blocks in your life. You've just got rid of one. I can help you to get rid of the other. You need money, Bruce. Enough money to be able to forget about food and rent until you're ready to write that big one. I can show you how to get it."

Cameron's fingers relaxed. In spite of himself he was strangely excited. "You can't imagine what you do to me. Who are you — a field man for the Huntington Hartford Awards?"

Thorne threw up his hands — color was back in his cheeks. He seemed sure of himself for the first time since Cameron had entered the house.

"I'm in business for Henry Thorne. Over the last ten years I've created the image of a respectable stamp dealer. It's an illusion. What *really* earns the money is burglary. That's what I am, Bruce, a highly skilled burglar."

Cameron tipped the decanter. He experienced no sense of moral shock — nothing more than increased excitement. It was as though he were being offered the key to a closed door. Beyond the door lay the chance of a lifetime. Yet turning the key might be dangerous. He looked over the top of his tumbler.

"Why do you find *me* so fascinating — because you've decided to marry my girlfriend?"

Thorne smiled bleakly. "Quality. Ambition. Enough imagination to realize that laws are made for fools. Others break them with impunity. I've already got one recruit — you could be the second. I know exactly where I'm going, make no mistakes about it. A year from now, you can have your island in the sun and write the book you always promised yourself."

For some reason or other Cameron's head had completely cleared. His pale blue eyes were guarded.

"I'm beginning to get the swing — life does go on and what's a woman between highwaymen? Is that what you're trying to say?"

Thorne held his hands to the fire. "More or less. I'm a realist. We can be of use to one another. The rest is nonsense. You've got to forget about Jamie and think of me as an ally. If your emotions trouble you, write them out — don't complicate your life with them."

Cameron lifted his tumbler to the light as if baffled by its emptiness.

"Harsh words for a prospective bridegroom."

Thorne smiled remotely. "*Nothing* complicates life except lack of money. If it's Jamie's future that's worrying you, forget about it. I won't let her down. We have an understanding."

Cameron put his glass on the table very carefully. *An understanding.* No matter how you looked at it, this is what she had left him for. "You just acquired another recruit," he said slowly.

Thorne walked over from the fireplace, hand out-stretched. "I don't think you'll regret it."

Cameron got to his feet. It seemed somehow logical to take Thorne's hand, give it the True-Blue treatment.

"Let's hope neither of us regrets it," he answered.

It was two o'clock in the morning when he left the house. He'd walked home in the snow. The empty flat was no longer lonely. He'd undressed, reflecting that biding his time was a maneuver he could learn. A month later Thorne and Jamie were married. In some strange way the marriage set a seal on his association with Thorne. A strange guarded association with each aware of the final challenge to come. Two weeks after that, Thorne initiated him into the niceties of burglary. His onetime relationship with Jamie was never mentioned. It was all very sophisticated and more than a year ago.

He turned the corner and hurried west on King's Road. The streets were empty, save for the occasional car ploughing slush onto the sidewalks. The hell with her. The hell with everything but the money. It was what he had gone into this thing for. He'd do better if he kept his values sharply defined.

HENRY CADWALLADER THORNE
22nd December

T HE BEDROOM was a disgrace — a shambles. Her bloody shoes lay on the floor where she had kicked them off. She'd left a pair of stockings draped over the dressing-table mirror — magazines and a half-chewed apple in the cat's basket. The radio was still playing — she'd forgotten it hours ago. Handles were missing from the drawers. Wood surfaces that had been polished for generations had become dull and scarred. She'd even broken the hinges on the linen chest in some weird experiment in stress and strain.

He turned off the radio and groped under the bed for a cheap canvas bag bought in a multiple store. He packed the tracksuit, gloves and shoes — emptied his pockets except for some loose change and a couple of pounds.

His nose wrinkled as he went through into the bathroom. God, she was a slut! Underclothes dripped from a drying frame suspended over the tub. The one surviving goldfish floated dispiritedly over the pebbles at the bottom of its tank. He changed the water and sprinkled a pinch of ant's eggs on the surface. The briefing session couldn't have gone better. They'd reacted exactly as he'd expected. Robin's last-minute demand had been typical. And Bruce had been his surly self. "Mystery X" was the only one who hadn't shown his hand. The derisive nickname Gunn had given him no longer irritated — in fact it amused him. "Mystery X" was precisely what he was — the unknown quantity — unknown to them, to Jamie and to the police. Unknown in fact to everyone except himself. While they had no secrets from him — Robin's dream, for instance, was to find himself in some smart resort thronged with women anxious to leap into bed with him; Cameron was a secret sentimentalist whose one idea of happiness was Jamie beside him in the sunshine, a sounding board for the death, doom and disaster nonsense he thought was good writing.

He scrubbed his nails carefully, satisfied that his own plans were less romantic. Fantasy played no part in his life. All he needed was a country that would be receptive to his arrival — a place where intelligence and sixty thousand pounds could be employed to his lasting benefit. As for Jamie — she could go on traveling whichever way the wind blew, living on her charm. It would be interesting to see how long the charm held up.

He brushed his sandy hair into a neat cap, picked up the bag and went downstairs. He closed the sitting room window. The wind outside had dropped. He chucked the two spools of film on the fire where they flared briefly. The pans and chemicals he'd used to develop the films were safely ditched miles away. He dropped the bag in the hall and went through to the kitchen.

Jamie was sitting at the table, holding the cat on her lap. He smiled and made the sort of face and noise expected of him.

"I'm off, darling. I should be back about eight. I thought we might eat out somewhere. Would you like that?"

She took the gold buckle out of her hair. The mass of butter-blond hair swung across her eyes. She pushed it away impatiently.

"What did *they* want?"

He picked the cat from her arms. It kneaded its claws in his sleeve. The sensuous purr gave him a feeling of comradeship. Benjie's only real interest was in himself. He poured the cat a saucer of cream, wondering how to answer her. The house would be full of police in the morning. He wanted Jamie to deal with their questions truthfully and without floundering. He shrugged.

"They wanted the car but I need it myself. Why?"

She nibbled a piece of skin on her finger. "Every time Robin comes to the house it's to borrow something. Money — the car — even the field glasses. I wish you wouldn't have him here."

He made the slightest sound of deprecation. "He's a friend of mine."

She raised her eyes. "He's nobody's friend."

He was careful to keep his voice casual. "How about Bruce — don't you want him here either?"

59

She answered deliberately. "No, Henry, I don't want Bruce here either."

She took his wrist in her hand as he touched her cheek, and held it tight. He looked down at her.

"I was only joking. But it is your house as much as it's mine. The people who come here are your guests. All I'm trying to suggest is that you could be polite to them. As I am — to your friends."

She let his wrist go. "What friends?"

It was a point. The odd girl from her art school days — a vague aunt who was her only relative. All right. Friends she might not have, but she certainly had a lover. The role of Caesar's wife was too big for her. He patted her cheek.

"You're being harsh on Robin. He's a snob and has the morals of a goat, but I find him amusing. He's got charm, and above all he's very useful. I've done a great deal of business through him — people he knows who've been left collections, that sort of thing."

She used a touch of his own manner. "What about Bruce — is he useful too?"

He watched the cat's steady lapping. "It's not the word. I'm not sure you're going to understand this, Jamie, but I have a very real feeling of responsibility for Bruce. It's one of the reasons I've encouraged him to come to the house since our marriage. The other is that he's a good writer — or could be — that's important. One of these days he's going to prove it — I'm convinced of that. Meanwhile I get a great deal of pleasure being able to help in a small way."

She made a gesture of dissent. "I've always known

that you felt guilty about what happened. It's wrong. It's wrong for me, for you, even for Bruce. We just can't go on like this, Henry. The whole thing's unnatural. You're too kind — too decent, I suppose — to see it."

He made the appropriate answer. "I'm not a jealous man, Jamie, if that's what you mean. Nor do I have any reason to be."

She shook her head despairingly. "Don't you *want* to understand? You're loyal, so you imagine everyone you believe in is loyal too."

He smiled again, wider this time and understandingly. "Aren't they?"

She added another plate to the pile in the sink and dribbled hot water on them.

"I give up. Not that I'd change you, darling. I want you to know that being your wife means more to me at this moment than anything else in the world." She poured soap powder into the hot water. Her voice sharpened. "You said you were helping Bruce — what was that supposed to mean?"

Instinct flooded his brain with caution. In that moment he was certain she knew more than she should. Cameron might have hinted that something was brewing. It wouldn't be more than a hint — Bruce wasn't that kind of a fool. A suggestion perhaps that soon they could be rid of *him*. He hitched a shoulder.

"Nothing very much. The odd fiver to help pay a bill. The name of a literary agent I met at a party. Bruce is a difficult chap to help. There's something perverse in his nature that makes it hard for him to accept favors. This deal he's been offered should put an end to all that." He waited for her to rise to the bait.

She did so, turning from the sink with dripping hands. "A deal? What sort of a deal? You mean something to do with Robin?"

He held both hands up in protest. "One question at a time! All I know is that they're both supposed to be going to make their fortunes. Something to do with property development. Robin has lots of contacts, and they've both got drive and imagination. It might well work. They seem very confident. I'm especially glad for Bruce. Money means time to write."

Her voice was very quiet. "And why didn't you let them take the car?"

"I told you, I need it myself. If you're worrying about their operational expenses, don't. I let them have fifty quid. It won't make or break us."

She circled his neck with her arms. "I love you, darling. Did anyone ever tell you that you're a good man?"

Her face was hidden against his shoulder. He smiled at his reflection in the kitchen mirror.

"Almost never. I've got to fly now, pet. I'll be back as near eight as I can make it. Let's try the 'Hungry Horse.' Why don't you book a table?"

She nodded, her eyes on him as he collected the bag from the hall. She clung to his hand till they reached the street door. He waved goodbye. The cobbles were slippery with freezing snow. He put up his collar and hurried to where he had left his car. He drove west, crossing Fulham Palace Road into a maze of monotonous streets. Rows of dirty brick dwellings were telescoped between shabby corner stores. Chimney smoke plumed through the television masts adding to the general gloom. He drove left, turning in between high blank walls. A corrugated-iron fence at the end formed an impasse. A tall pair of wooden doors were secured with a padlock. He glanced back through the rear window. Reassured, he left the car and went to the bottom of the wall. He groped about in the snow-covered weeds. The key was under a stone where he had left it. He undid the padlock and drove into the yard. The gates were secured on the inside by a balk of timber thrust through a couple of iron rings. More high walls enclosed the yard. The derelict factory building overlooked the river. He dragged the sagging doors open and drove the Opel into the warehouse. The interior was dark. Overhead was a half floor reached by a rotting stairway. An ancient crane perched there, its boom sticking out over the swollen water through a hole in the wall. The windows appeared to have been used as targets by a generation of sharpshooters on the towpath below.

He walked to the far end of the building. Another set of doors opened onto a side street a block away from where he had entered. He glanced down at the concrete floor. There were no tire marks — no oil patches — nothing to indicate that the fake laundry van had been hidden there. He changed into his tracksuit, leaving his street clothes in the station wagon.

He had found the abandoned warehouse months ago, one summer afternoon, fishing the stretch of river outside. It was one of half a dozen boltholes he had discovered by accident. They varied in type and in district. A condemned school, for instance, forgotten in inter-departmental squabbling. A West End theater awaiting development. While across the river in Battersea he knew of an entire block of houses, uninhabited and scheduled for demolition. The premises served as hiding places, changing rooms or vantage points. He knew every yard of the territory, the precautions to be taken in each district.

He checked his watch. It was a quarter to five. He strolled back to a door painted OFFICE. The dank room was empty except for a used tea chest. The top had been taken off and lay on the floor. The securing nails were half-pried from the wood. He tilted the case speculatively. It was lined with tinfoil. British Railways handled thousands like it every day. Its journey from Waterloo Station to the country would be uneventful. Nobody connected with Henry Thorne knew about the house in Weston. He'd had it for three years — a brick and timber farmhouse sitting in the middle of twenty acres of scrub timber. The handful of people living in the hamlet knew him as George Watson — a businessman from Southampton. George Watson's check had bought the property. George Watson paid the phone and electricity bills. George Watson's name appeared on the voter's list — a man who kept largely to himself. Other than the Warrens, his nearest neighbors, he knew no one except by sight. He fished the rivers on weekends and local curiosity had long since been exhausted.

He dragged the metal-bound case through the door. The virtue of his plan was its simplicity. They would drive back here and unload the payroll then the van would be dumped in the sandpits. He'd follow in his car, dropping Gunn and Cameron separately. He'd take the money to Waterloo in the station wagon. By then, every available squad car in the area would be roaring through the night, none of them knowing what they were looking for. The packing case would sit at Templecombe Station until George Watson called for it. No loose thinking there, friends Robin and Bruce — just old Mystery X at his most mysterious.

The next step was to convert the stolen money into safe currency. That was Kosky's department. Kosky was one of his own kind. A man without sentimental scruples and with the same refusal to be duped by appearances. It had been Kosky who supplied all the documentation for George Watson's identity. Even more important, Kosky had created Henry Turberville. It was all there in a bedroom in the farmhouse. Passport, birth certificate, driving license — family letters back-dated over the years. Twenty-four hours after Kosky had taken delivery of the payroll money, a numbered account in a Zurich bank would be available to Henry Turberville.

He went back and unbolted the end door. He wheeled the bicycle outside, pulled on a gray plastic cape and pedalled off in the direction of Hammersmith. After a mile he turned towards the river. The white van he expected to see was parked at the foot of the bridge. The traffic signals were against him. He propped himself against the curb with one foot, snow gathering in the folds of his cape, making his neck uncomfortable. A truck driver high and dry in his cab pantomimed mock sympathy. Amber changed to green. He pedalled over the bridge. The river curved below him. Far off to the east a span of lamps hung over the rushing water. The van overtook him. He put on speed going down the far slope of the bridge.

He headed for the pub on the corner and wheeled onto the asphalt parking lot. He was already out of the saddle as the van started reversing towards him. Cameron threw the doors open and pulled up the bicycle. Thorne scrambled after it. The only spectator of the transfer was a seagull that flew off squawking.

Thorne felt his way forward to the hatch behind the driver's seat. A peaked cap was pulled over Gunn's eyes. He was wearing a white coat with the name AJAX LAUNDRY SERVICE embroidered in red lettering. He wrestled with the wheel, wrenching the van out of a four-wheel skid. Its course straightened. He drove fast, following the line of the river towards Chiswick.

Thorne lurched as the van swayed. "Slower!" he shouted. "Or you'll have us up on the pavement!"

Gunn's eyes were fixed on the shining strip unwinding into the headlamps.

"Sit down and let me do the driving," he said over his shoulder.

Cameron's hand touched Thorne's sleeve in warning. Two of the three hampers were open. The basketwork hinges had been cut through so that the lids could be lifted in inverse fashion. Once shut from the inside, the hampers would be proof against any cursory inspection.

Cameron and Thorne crouched as the van stopped at an intersection. Lights from the passing vehicles swept through the hatch, passing over their doubled bodies. The van forked right onto a stretch of freeway. Thorne lifted himself on one knee. A red sign was coming up ahead, blinking its message:

HALL'S****THE****HOME****
OF****GOOD****FURNITURE

The factory gates were wide open, the building beyond them brilliantly lighted. Thorne leaned through the hatch.

"Where the hell's Seager?"

Gunn braked hard. "For Christ's sake stop breathing down my neck! Over there on the right — the small gray car."

A man sitting behind the wheel raised his hand. Gunn dipped his lamps in acknowledgment. He trod on the accelerator.

"We're almost there. I'm closing the hatch."

Thorne stepped into one of the hampers. He sat down, hugging his knees. Cameron dropped the lid on him. It was completely dark inside the hamper. It creaked with his weight. He smelled petrol fumes.

67

The two spare cans were wedged between the hamper and the side of the van. He had a sudden feeling of claustrophobia. There were nearly two more miles to go. He started counting the seconds. Suddenly the van swung round in a turn. His hamper skidded a foot. He heard the horn beep a couple of times — a man's voice answer Gunn's hail. The van stopped with the motor running. The exhaust pipe was clattering under the floorboards. Thorne tried to make his breathing as shallow as possible. The next seconds were decisive. If Seager hadn't done his job properly, the real driver could come on the phone at any minute — explaining to the gatekeeper why he couldn't make delivery. Thorne lay quite still, gripping his knees with his hands. He heard the gates being opened then Cameron's voice. He pushed up the top of the hamper. Cameron had already freed himself. They crouched side by side in the darkness. Gunn braked. Cameron wrenched the back doors open.

The motor died as they jumped out. The van was parked behind a low concrete building with windowless walls. A giant billboard hid them from the gatelodge. A couple of hundred yards away lights shone in the main blocks. A high-power lamp illuminated the steel door facing them. They went to work with the precision of a drill squad. Gunn and Cameron lifted a hamper from the back of the van while Thorne attacked the strongroom door. He'd notched the three skeleton keys with a file. His thumbnail found the nick he wanted. He guided the key into the narrow lock and turned his wrist. The door swung inward soundlessly. They pulled the hamper inside and shut the door. He switched on the light. The room was the size of a tennis court and sealed tight as a tomb. The air was flat and vitiated. Steel bars set in floor and ceiling divided the building in two. A long plank table near them was stacked with empty pay envelopes. Beyond the bars and in the far corner was a construction of solid steel, twenty feet square. A massive gate connected both halves of the room. Thorne went down on his knees. The bars were wide enough to allow the passage of his arm as far as the bicep. He felt round till his fingers found the hidden switch. The burglar alarm was connected to the local police station. It remained switched on whenever there was money in the strongroom. The only danger was that one of the staff might have been careless about the on-off positions. Throwing the switch might be making the contact instead of breaking it. Someone touched his shoulder. He looked up. The Canadian's face was glistening. He tightened his grip.

"Throw it," he said. "What the hell are you waiting for?"

Thorne thumbed the switch down. He used the second key on the ponderous gate. They dragged the hamper across the floor to the solid steel vault. The last of the three keys had wards on each side of its short thick barrel. He eased it into the lock with the delicacy of a surgeon, supporting the shank with his left forefinger. The key revolved slowly, engaging the tumblers. He turned it one full circle then repeated the maneuver in the opposite direction. He withdrew the key and pushed. The door rolled back on an oiled carriageway. He wiped the back of his neck. The wire racks in front of them were stacked with rows of banknotes. Each row had a typewritten card propped against the end. He counted them. Twelve by five plus one equaled sixty-one. Seager's information was crack-on. Cameron seemed stunned by the sight of the money. He leaned against the racks, fanning himself with his hand.

"You take the left — I'll take the right," said Thorne.

They worked hurriedly, packing the notes into the hamper and carried it to the outside door. Thorne locked the vault and gate. He cut off the light, opened the door and peeked outside. The overhead lamp threw a brilliant arc as far as the shadows where the van was parked. He gestured with his hand. Gunn came out of the snow, his voice hoarse.

"We're behind time already!"

They hoisted the hamper into the back of the van. Gunn raced the motor nervously. The two men behind climbed into their baskets and lowered the lids. Thorne crouched, listening to the whine of the differential. Once they were past the gatelodge they were safe. The genuine laundry van would arrive at any moment. And hell would break loose. According to Seager there were only two authorized sets of keys to the strongroom — the company secretary had one — the other was kept in the bank. It would take time to get at either. And until they did, nobody connected with the place could be sure what they had lost — or if they'd lost anything. The van stopped.

Slow footsteps were followed by a surly voice; "Took yer time up there, didn't you? I dunno — some of you youngsters don't know what a day's work is."

Gunn made no reply. The man's grumble faded as he pushed the gates open. Gunn revved the motor. The van was shot forward as if kicked from behind. It turned in a tight half circle and gathered more speed. Thorne wrestled out of his hamper. Cameron had beaten him to it. They leaned through the open hatch. Gunn's face grinned from the driving mirror.

"We've done it — we've bloody well done it!" he said exultantly. The speedmeter needle was nudging sixty.

Cameron steadied himself with both hands. "Then let's go on living so we can talk about it." The van's speed slackened. Thorne was watching the road ahead. A truck was hugging the crown of the highway, its tail lamps almost obscured by diesel fumes. Gunn sounded his horn impatiently. The truck pulled over. The flashing sign of the furniture factory loomed ahead. Gunn put his foot down hard as they passed the entrance.

"Did you see the van? It was on its way down. A couple more minutes and we'd have met." He seemed amused by the idea.

They shot under the airport freeway, the exhaust thundering in the tunnel. The Chiswick streets were well lit, the shops warm oases in the swirling snow.

Gunn wheeled the van east, across the traffic, bluffing his way through the oncoming vehicles. They rolled down the short approach to the river. A bluish blaze from the brewery lit the opposite bank, silhouetting the deserted warehouse. Thorne jumped out and opened the doors. Gunn drove the van into the warehouse. Nobody spoke — each man knowing what he had to do and doing it with hurried competence. Thorne unloaded the hamper. Cameron was already bolting another license plate on the front end of the van. Gunn stripped the adhesive lettering from its side, wiped the surface with a gasolined rag and pressed on a new emblem. It now read:

BRENT BROTHERS LANDSCAPE DESIGNERS

They changed into their street clothes, throwing the tracksuits in the back of the van. Thorne looked at the time. Twenty past six. He walked across to Gunn, holding the strongroom keys in his outstretched hand. He wanted both of them to see them.

"Dump these in the pond with the bicycle. Everything else will burn — we'd better get going."

Gunn dropped the keys into a pocket, his elegant self in a blue cashmere overcoat, white silk scarf.

"Don't get too far behind. You might be lonely."

The Canadian was leaning against the radiator of Thorne's car. He shook his head slowly.

"He won't be lonely. I'm riding with him."

A barge hooted upstream. The sound echoed over

their heads. Thorne shrugged. He threw Cameron a brand new padlock.

"Suit yourself, Bruce. Make sure that lock's properly on."

He moved the station wagon out into the street, keeping its motor running as Cameron snapped the padlock through the hoops. The van waited twenty yards ahead. Cameron walked over. Something about his manner — his apparent assuredness — gave Thorne the feeling that he might have forgotten something vital to his plan. He checked the dash gauges purely from habit. The readings were normal. Cameron opened the door and took the seat beside Thorne. He let the padlock key drop into Thorne's lap.

Thorne shifted into the bottom gear. The conviction was growing that the other had a scheme of his own under weigh. The clue lay with Jamie — that was certain. The answer hit like a hammer. Cameron's plan was the same as his own — to bolt with the whole of the Palaton payroll — and Jamie as well. It all fell into place. The Canadian's fake allegiance about the disposal of the money — the act Jamie had put on after he'd left.

He touched the accelerator, keeping his eyes on the van. It turned into the westbound stream of traffic. Now and then he checked the driving mirror. The substitution of vans might still be undetected, but they weren't out of the danger zone. It sounded as if the same thought was troubling Cameron.

"It's too soon for them to be on to us — or isn't it?"

Thorne steered into the outside lane. Gunn was getting too far ahead. He sneaked a look at the man beside him. Cameron's expression afforded no hint of anything but a mild interest in the traffic.

"They're looking for another van — another number — if they *are* looking," said Thorne. "There's something I wanted to say, Bruce — I'm a bit worried about Robin. I've got a feeling that he's going to be awkward about the money when it comes to it. We're still on the same side, aren't we?"

Cameron turned his head lazily. "Always, Henry, you know that."

Thorne cut out, blocking off a cab intent on coming between him and the van. "I'm glad. I've relied on you all the way through. At least we think the same way."

The lines deepened round Cameron's mouth. "About one subject, friend. Watch that truck."

Six miles on, the van turned off the highway. Another mile and they were bumping down a lane between fields. Birds rose from the hedgerows, disturbed by their passage. The snowfall had stopped. The night was still and cold with a low-bellied sky. They traveled at walking pace, past bare trees standing in isolation. The lane was slippery with frozen mud. It twisted suddenly, revealing a gate that barred their way. Red lights glowed as the van stopped.

Gunn walked back, swinging his arms to keep warm. He leaned through Thorne's window grinning.

"I hope you recognized the hand of the maestro.

Twenty-six minutes dead. We've made up the time we lost."

He showed them an upturned thumb, strolled away and pulled the gate back. He drove into the quarry. Thorne took off the handbrake letting the car roll down the incline. Twenty feet below was a pond covered with a thin skin of ice. Cameron perched himself on a front fender. They watched Gunn maneuver the van down the deep cut leading to the sandpits. He wheeled the bicycle to the edge of the pool. Lifting it high over his head, he hurled it away from him. It broke through the ice. Water plumed. Ripples slapped against the sides of the pit. Gunn swung his arm again. There was a smaller splash as he found the same spot with the keys.

A night bird screamed somewhere behind them. It was like watching a performance in an amphitheater. Gunn's silhouette, the outline of the van, were clear against the background of light sand. He walked round to the rear of the vehicle carrying a can of gasoline in each hand. He spilled fuel round each tire, tipped an entire can into the back of the van and shut the doors. He started walking backwards, dribbling a trail from the second can as he went. Then he squatted on his haunches. They saw the match flare in his cupped hands.

The flash was sudden and dramatic. It lit the sandpits from one end to the other. The fire that followed ran too swiftly for the eye. A brilliant sheet of flame enveloped the van simultaneous with a violent explosion. Gunn sprang to his feet. He wheeled and moved forward. One foot caught. He stumbled on, still holding the gasoline can against his stomach. They watched, powerless to help, as the fuel ran over his body. It linked with the train of fire he had laid. He pulled himself upright again, screaming as the flames reached his head. He broke for the water in an ugly shamble, clawing at his face. He covered no more than a dozen yards then collapsed. He was lying flat on his stomach, blue flames still licking his shoulders. The van had settled down to a steady blaze. Metal was buckling under the intensity of the heat. From lighted match to disaster had taken no more than ten seconds.

Both men came to life at the same time. They slid down the side of the pit and ran towards the still form lying on the ground. Cameron was first to reach it. He turned Gunn over gently. Charred clothing came away in his fingers. There was a strong smell of singed hair. Little of it was left on Gunn's skull. The flesh across his cheeks was black, his burned lips drawn back in a snarl. Even his eyelids were seared. A high pitched scream was coming from his nose and mouth.

Cameron whipped off his raincoat. He wrapped it round the top half of Gunn's body. The glare from the burning van lit the horror on the Canadian's face.

"Get hold of his feet!" he shouted. "Get hold of his feet, goddammit!"

Thorne bent down, battling with his revulsion. They lifted Gunn, slipping as they climbed the icy slope. They laid him in the back of the station wagon shrouded in Cameron's coat. His breathing came in a choked gurgle.

Thorne sat behind the wheel with shaking hands. Cameron reached across and switched on the ignition.

"Get out of here fast," he ordered.

Thorne put the car in gear. He drove mechanically, his brain spinning through one possibility after another. They'd be on the main highway in a few more seconds — with lighted streets, busses with top-deck passengers staring down into the station wagon. He braked suddenly and killed the motor.

"We'll have to get rid of him."

Cameron's head was between his hands. He lifted it slowly.

"*What* did you say?"

"I said it's suicidal lunacy." He gave one reason after another, eagerly. "We can't take him to hospital. They'd want names and addresses. There's always a cop hanging around. We wouldn't have a hope."

Cameron's eyes narrowed. "And what do you suggest?"

Instinct told Thorne not to answer. But his eyes did it for him.

"You dirty murderous bastard," Cameron said with cold hate.

Thorne shrugged. Cameron climbed over the back of the seat — he looked down at Gunn, his face hidden — he covered the lower half of the injured man's body with Thorne's dufflecoat.

"Move over," he ordered.

He took Thorne's place behind the wheel and switched on the motor. "We're going to get him to a doctor. You start thinking where."

The snow lay an inch thick on the main highway. Cameron drove fast, whipping through his gears savagely. He forked right at the first set of traffic signals. A secondary road ran them into the back reaches of Hammersmith. Thorne sat bolt upright, saying nothing. All he had to do was to keep his head. Maybe Bruce didn't realize it, but his number was up. The signals turned red. Cameron eased the wagon onto the crown of the highway. A cabdriver on their left looked across, scanning the inside of the wagon incuriously. Cameron's snarl took some of the edge off Thorne's renewed confidence.

"OK. What about it — a doctor who won't ask questions!"

Thorne already had the answer. A crooked cop — a false passport — a back way out of the country. Kosky provided everything at a price.

"I know someone who'll help. I'll have to get to a phone."

Cameron was intent on the traffic signals. "We'll take him to your place."

"That's out," Thorne said quickly. "There's a girl staying the night — a friend of Jamie's."

"Then he'll have to go to Oakley Street." Cameron's voice hardened. "Where's the doctor?"

Thorne pointed at the changing lights. "I don't

know yet. But there's someone who'll know of one. Someone reliable."

Cameron engaged gear. "He'd better be. For your sake he'd better be."

The car moved forward, filtering into the eastbound traffic moving towards the bridge. He pulled up at the end of the cul-de-sac. It was quiet. The wind whipped off the river, rattling the palings guarding the enbankment. The bustle of Hammersmith Broadway seemed very far away.

Cameron jerked his head. "Open the doors — you've got the key."

Thorne did as he was told. The warehouse was alive with sounds of its own. When he went in, the Canadian was waiting in the light from the headlamps.

"Robin was right. We'll cut the money up tonight. Just like that?" He could think of nothing else to say.

Cameron's long shadow moved on the whitewashed wall.

"Just like that," he said.

Thorne shaded his eyes from the light. "I don't suppose it matters. The way we're going we'll never have a chance to spend it."

The Canadian walked round to the back of the wagon. The remark seemed to have made no impression on him.

"Someone'll have to get hold of Robin's mother."

"I will," Thorne said quickly. A new plan was shaping in his mind.

Cameron unfastened the tailgate. He dropped it

and peered in at the huddled figure. He hauled the tea chest over to the station wagon. Thorne helped lift it into the back. Cameron knelt down. He bared Gunn's head, his voice gentle.

"Move your hand if you can hear me, Robin."

Both men watched intently as the fingers of Gunn's left hand jerked apart. Cameron bent lower over the ravaged face.

"You're going to my place, Robin. I promise you won't be left. You're going to be all right — everything's going to be all right. We're cutting the money up tonight. I'll get a doctor to you as soon as I can. But there's something I've got to do first — something to keep you quiet. Do you understand?"

It looked as if Gunn were fighting for breath. His eyes opened wide and fixed Cameron. His fingers barely moved.

Cameron reached across the bench seat and yanked out the ignition keys. He cut the headlamps. Thorne heard the door scrape over the cement floor. Gunn stirred in the darkness. Thorne moved away instinctively. Two thoughts dominated his brain. The money and the letter he'd mailed three hours before. Somehow he had to move himself and the packing case down to Weston. He sat up as the door was dragged open again. Cameron climbed into the wagon and switched on the dashlight. He ripped the paper wrapping from a half bottle of whiskey and went down on his knees. He held the bottle up so that Gunn could see it.

"Come on, kid," he urged, "open your mouth."

Gunn's eyes rolled. The effort required seemed beyond him.

Cameron pried Gunn's jaws apart. He wedged the cork between the other man's teeth and tipped the bottle. The whiskey spilled out of Gunn's mouth, running over the raw flesh at the bottom of his nostrils. Tears oozed from the tightly shut eyes. The bottle was empty. Cameron lifted the prostrate body, placing it so that it lay lengthwise behind the seat. He covered it completely with the coats. Anyone looking into the car from the outside would see no more than a shapeless bundle. He walked across the warehouse and pitched the empty bottle through a broken window.

He came back, took his place behind the wheel and sat with his forehead resting against his hands. He shook himself suddenly as if he had been doused with cold water.

"You've cut all your corners," he said in a sandpaper voice. "Don't make any mistake about it, Henry."

Thorne blinked. "You're talking in riddles. You wanted a doctor — all right, I'm going to get one. But if you want to sleep in your own bed tonight — if you want to be able to spend your share of the money — you'd better listen to what I'm saying. Some of the numbers of those notes are definitely known to the police. While we're sitting here, they're being run off on a duplicating machine. The broadsheets'll be in every hotel, restaurant and nightclub by tomorrow morning. Every bank in the country will have a record of the numbers. What do *you* propose to do — make the rounds of the betting shops, changing up tenners? With half a dozen stoolpigeons running for the nearest phone?"

Cameron's eyes were watchful. But his silence encouraged Thorne. Two things were essential to his change of plan — speed and sacrifice. He had less than ten hours in which to work. First he had to retrieve the evidence he'd planted and then get down to Somerset. With luck they could be there before midnight.

The cops would raid the three addresses in the morning and find nothing. They'd blame the anonymous letter on some crank or other and go about their business.

Jamie, he thought suddenly. If he could get her *and* Cameron down to the country he'd be that much surer of them both. He pushed his hand into the glove compartment and held the label to the light. He read the typewritten address aloud:

> *Mr. George Watson*
> *Templecombe Goods Station*
> TO BE CALLED FOR

Cameron made no response, withdrawn and suspicious.

"*I'm* George Watson," said Thorne. I've got a farmhouse not far from Templecombe. A place called Weston. I've had it three years. It isn't even a village, just a church and half a dozen cottages. The nearest cop's stationed six miles away. He *salutes* me, Bruce. I give him trout flys and buy raffle tickets from him. Once that case is on the train there isn't a cop in the world who'll trace it."

He waited for Cameron to say something. Kosky would send someone down to collect the money within hours. Everything that Thorne needed was already in the farmhouse. Passport, clothes, airplane ticket. He could be in Zurich in twenty-four hours leaving Jamie and Cameron wondering what had hit them. He'd already dismissed Gunn from his calculations.

The car started creeping forward slowly. "Open the doors," Cameron said suddenly. Thorne obeyed. The short stretch of street was deserted. He waved Cameron outside and snapped the padlock back in place. The snow blew in flurries, obscuring the lights a hundred yards away. He took his place beside Cameron. Something about the Canadian's manner gave him renewed confidence. The aggressiveness was still there, but underneath was a hint of anxiety.

"How long would it take to get to this place of yours?"

Thorne pushed his behind deeper into the upholstery. "We could be there by midnight — one o'clock at the latest. We can leave as soon as we get hold of the doctor. We could even take him *with* us, Bruce. There are four bedrooms. No neighbors nearer than half a mile away."

Cameron touched the gas pedal. The motor raced. "We'll have to do something about his mother."

Thorne made the most of it. "I'll go and see her — think up some story that'll keep her quiet." What he had to do in reality was get her out of her flat with a fake emergency call. Five minutes alone in there was all that he needed.

Cameron's jaw muscles tightened. "OK. We'll do it your way. But don't make me nervous, Henry."

The parcels office was located underneath the main station building. Cameron pulled up outside and cut the radio. It had been playing ever since they had left the warehouse. Neither of the two wave bands mentioned the Palaton robbery. The nearest street lamp was yards away. Its light fell across the engine hood. The back of the station wagon was in darkness. Cameron glanced behind. Gunn was lying still under the huddle of coats.

"Let's go," he said, stepped over the seat and undid the tailgate. He took a hand trolley propped against the wall and held it while Thorne lowered the packing case.

"You take it in," he said. "I'll stay and watch the car."

Thorne pushed the trolley into the parcels office. The room was dim and dusty, lit by lamps fixed high in the ceiling. A mound of assorted freight was piled behind the counter. There was a strong smell of cheese about the place. He lifted a flap in the counter.

A porter broke away from a group sitting on a pile of mailbags, hand outstretched.

"Leave it there, mate, leave it there! This side of the counter's for staff only."

His comrades stiffened expectantly. He took the trolley from Thorne, ponderous with importance. An institutional clock hung over a desk against the wall. He consulted the clock before tipping the case onto a weigh-machine. His eyes measured the girth of the case. His face registered slight disappointment, as if yet another piece of merchandise had sneaked past his vigilance.

He dealt the side of the box a flat-handed blow, not bothering to read the typewritten labels.

"Where's it going, then?"

"Templecombe." There was no sense making the man still more hostile.

The porter walked flat-footedly to the desk. His friends had fallen silent, responsive to the display of authority given for their amusement. The minutes passed as the porter flipped through various batches of official papers on his desk. Thorne's voice was particularly patient.

"I'd like to get this case off tonight if it's possible."

"I daresay you would," the porter answered. He was having trouble with his sibilants. He sucked hard on a tooth and expectorated the result. The maneuver appeared to have been beneficial. "I daresay you would," he repeated, more clearly.

The clock ticked on. "*Is* it possible?" asked Thorne.

The man's hand described an arc that took in a hillock of trunks, bags, bicycles. Cases of groceries. Burlap-wrapped bundles.

"They're *all* in a hurry. We're two days away from Christmas and short 'anded. There's other people has holidays, you know." The sally drew a laugh from his friends.

"Hey!" Thorne swung round. Cameron had come to the door. He was looking at the porter, his eyes and mouth hostile. "What are you supposed to be," he asked. "Handling freight or the station clown?"

The porter's face reddened. "You watch your language, mate. Or I'll have you off the premises. This is England yer in and don't forget it."

Thorne broke in hurriedly. "All I want is to get this case down to Somerset the quickest way possible. Isn't there such a thing as an express service?"

The porter's glare followed Cameron outside. "Of course there is. But it ain't going to do you much good this time of the year, is it? We ain't allowed to guarantee *no* goods'll be on time."

Thorne folded a pound note. He dropped it on the desk just out of sight of the man's comrades. The porter's fist closed on it. He cleared a space for his elbow, repeating the address aloud as he wrote. He put his pen down.

"I'll do me best, but I can't promise nothing." He spoke loudly but his eyes narrowed perceptibly. He rose and trolleyed the packing case to the far end of the office. The two men climbed to the mainline station. As they neared the top of the steps Thorne felt Cameron's fingers close on his sleeve. The vast hall was thronged. People were sleeping in front of the Departure Board, their feet resting on upturned suitcases, deaf to the hubbub about them. Elderly couples with patient faces clutched string bags loaded with food. A drunk was snoring on an elbow. Pigeons roosted high on the girders supporting the glass dome. A row of telephones lined one of the booking halls. Cameron's fingers tightened. He steered Thorne into an empty booth and shoved the receiver into his hand. "The doctor," he said.

Thorne pushed a coin into the slot and dialed. The buzzer rang. He hung up and dialed again. He repeated the maneuver a third time, each time letting the number ring. A man's voice answered immediately, cautious and guttural.

"Kosky."

Thorne spoke in fluent German. "Ja, hier ist Heinrich. Ich bin gut zu hause gekommen."

Kosky's voice was fat with a sort of avuncular approval. "Well done," he said. "Well done. Then we shall be seeing one another as arranged?"

Thorne looked up at Cameron. They were wedged into the booth facing one another. The Canadian's cheek was twitching, his eyes wary.

"That's right," Thorne said carefully. "If there's any change I'll notify you personally. Is that clear?"

Kosky wheezed into a whisper. "Is there something the matter — are you alone?"

Thorne felt apprehensive suddenly — as if Cameron was only biding his time to spring something to which even Kosky had no answer.

"No," he said slowly. "No I'm not. There's been an accident and I need help." He screwed his eyes up at Cameron, pantomiming the need for patience.

Kosky grunted. "An accident — what *sort* of accident?"

Cameron was still watching closely, his shoulders blocking the way out. Thorne coaxed into the mouth-piece.

"Not what you're thinking. A man's been burned. I want a doctor — *our* sort of doctor. Don't worry about the money part of it. Just get things moving."

The line was muffled as if someone had covered the receiver at the other end. Then Kosky was back.

"Listen carefully. You must go to Paul Street, May-fair. Number seventy-seven. It is a club called the Mandrake. Ask for Mr. Chalice. C–h–a–l–i–c–e. He will be expecting you. He is quite reliable. Till tomorrow evening, then, unless I hear to the contrary. Auf wiederhören."

"Auf wiederhören," Thorne repeated mechanically and hung up. Cameron pushed the door of the booth. Thorne stepped out wiping his forehead.

"It's all fixed. They're going to have a doctor waiting. I told you."

"Waiting *where?*" The outside edge of the Canadian's hostility showed again.

Thorne's tongue licked the corners of his mouth. "I've got to go to a club in Shepherd's Market." He almost fell as Cameron spun him round. "You better be going, Henry!"

A woman with a child passed, looking at them curiously. Thorne freed himself, laughing for her benefit.

"For God's sake cut it out," he pleaded. "People are looking at us. Let's get moving. The club's just a meeting place."

They hurried down to the parked station wagon. As far as Thorne could see, the figure under the pile of coats hadn't changed position. The starter kicked life into the motor. Cameron held out his hand.

"Give me that receipt. The one they gave you for the packing case."

Thorne shook his head. "How do you expect to go on like this? You don't trust anything I do or say."

Cameron crooked his finger. "Just give the paper. I'm doing my best to keep an open mind about you. Don't make it too tough." Thorne surrendered the slip. There were a lot of cards to play yet — from his hand and from his sleeve. The one thing that was sure was that Cameron wasn't going anywhere without Jamie. Wherever you started you always came back to her.

Oakley Street was a cold and blustery canyon where art students washed their hair behind drawn curtains. In other rooms Hindus prepared intricately argued theses — camp young men quarreled violently about who had been responsible for the previous night's bitchiness. It was a street whose promise was tinged with sadness.

Cameron pulled on the handbrake and cut the motor. "Stay where you are — I'll go open the door."

He went down the steps with practiced speed. He was back within seconds, stopping just below street level. He looked first right and then left. A few people were loitering at the bus stop a hundred yards away. Off in the other direction a man and woman were walking a fat dog stuffed into a woolen jacket. Cameron hurried across the sidewalk and started undoing the back of the station wagon. As he leaned the top half of his body into the car a door slammed behind him. A girl came out of the house. She added an empty milk bottle to the collection at the top of the steps and looked down, her attention drawn to the parked car. Cameron's attempt to conceal himself came too late. Her heels rattled across the sidewalk. He went to meet her, putting himself between her and the car. She was young and eager — a brunette in a houndstooth check coat with a black velvet collar. She flashed a smile at him.

"Bruce! I *thought* it was you! Your phone's been ringing for the last half hour. I tried to get in to answer, but the key wasn't in the usual place."

Cameron wrapped an arm round her shoulders and led her a few yards up the street. They were near enough for Thorne to hear the conversation.

"I wouldn't worry. Probably some bill collector."

She wriggled free and looked back at the parked car. Thorne ducked his head hurriedly. The girl pivoted on the heel of a black pump.

"More likely some woman, or have you given them up *too*?"

Cameron was tall in the light from the street lamp. His grin was strained.

"Not as long as you're around."

The small cat's face smiled back at him. "Liar. But you could do a lot worse. I'm housetrained, earn my own living and very affectionate."

Cameron patted her rump. "And also out of my age group. Anyway I've got two heads. You wouldn't like the other one."

She turned down the corners of her mouth and stuck out her tongue at him. The lamplight showed something hard creep into his face. He watched her to the end of the street and walked back to Thorne's side of the car. "Let's go! And make it look natural we're putting a drunk to bed."

He lifted Gunn's body. The coats slipped as Thorne took his share of the weight. Gunn's eyelids were shut tight. Spittle dribbled from the corner of his mouth. Thorne looked away, repelled in spite of himself.

"*Lift*, you bastard," Cameron said harshly. "You fall apart on me now and I'll kill you."

They lugged Gunn over the tailgate and hoisted him on his feet. Each took an arm over his shoulder. His head rolled as if his neck were broken. His feet dragged. He showed a sign of life only once — a deep groan as they went down the steps. Cameron kicked open the door. The reek of Scotch and burned flesh was even stronger now they were inside the house. Thorne closed his nostrils and took a fresh grip. They half-carried, half-dragged Gunn down the passage. They laid him on the bed. Cameron bent down, flickering his thumb and forefinger near Gunn's ear. "Robin!"

Gunn's eyes seemed to creak open. His slack mouth bubbled. Cameron bent lower. "You're in my place, Robin — Oakley Street. We're going for a doctor, OK?"

The eyes whitened and then closed again. Cameron tore off a glove. He held Gunn's wrist, his face worried. Suddenly he straightened up and hitched his shoulders. "Let's get that doctor in a hurry." Someone emptied a bath upstairs, the waste gurgling in the outside plumbing. A bus rumbled by. Thorne took the shaving mirror from the tallboy. He walked three leaden steps to the side of the bed, and held the mirror against Gunn's lips.

"He's still breathing."

The lines deepened on Cameron's face. He pushed his fingers through short springy hair. "You do until you die."

He rearranged the pillows on the bed and turned the lamp so that Gunn's face was in shadow.

Thorne wet his mouth. "I think I'm going to be sick," he said unsteadily. He walked into the bathroom and shut the door. He dared not lock it. He flushed the water cistern, opened the kitchen door and tiptoed over to the oven. He forced his hand down between the frame and the metal lining, till his fingers found the keys he had hidden. He just managed to reach the sink as the light was switched on. Cameron was watching from the doorway. Thorne raised the glass of water.

"I *was* sick."

From the corner of his eye he could see that the oven door was open. The keys were heavy in his pocket. Cameron was wearing his mac. He threw Thorne's coat on the table and kicked the oven shut without even looking at it.

"With a mind like yours a weak stomach must be a handicap," he said.

Thorne wiped his mouth with the back of his hand. His brain always shed shock quicker than his muscle and nerve. He was still able to think faster than Cameron. He had the keys now for the map. Cameron came across to the sink. He screwed the faucet tight and reached into his raincoat pocket. When he turned round, he was holding a short-barreled automatic.

"Take a good look, Henry. I was never much of a shot but I'm not likely to miss at this range. Get your coat on."

The snowfall had stopped momentarily, but the low cloudless sky looked threatening. Cameron turned the ignition key, looked at his watch and switched on the radio. The voice in the speaker was mannered and impersonal.

"First the weather forecast. The cold weather will continue throughout the southern half of the country.

Temperatures generally will fall below freezing point. There will be fresh outbreaks of snow on high ground. The nine o'clock news follows almost immediately." There was still no mention of the robbery.

Cameron silenced the set. He looked down at the darkened basement flat. He seemed about to say something but changed his mind and headed the car north towards King's Road. He cut through Belgravia, crossed the park and turned down Curzon Street. He stopped opposite the hoop of Archway leading to the Shepherd's Market and put his hat on.

"Don't forget . . ." he started wearily then stopped. He shook his head. "What the hell — you won't."

The house had a Regency front with an iron coach-lamp hanging over the transom. Sober paint and discreetly drawn curtains combined in an impression of impeccable respectability. A pica-type sign in gilt proclaimed:

MANDRAKE *manor members only*

Thorne put is thumb on the button. A buzzer sounded. Someone inside operated an electrical circuit which released the door catch. They stepped into a hallway paneled in light pine. Bokhara runners were vivid on the parquet floor. Straight ahead was a flight of gray carpeted stairs. The sound of voices and music was loud behind the door on their left. Thorne pressed a second buzzer. The door was thrown open swiftly to let them in. It was closed just as quickly, blocking their exit. The man responsible for the maneuver was in his mid-twenties. His short fudge-colored hair was combed forward on a smallish head. He had flat ears and neat even features. He was wearing suede trousers, pigskin shoes and an Italian sweater. He gestured with a glass of tomato juice.

"Can't you geezers read? This is a members' club. Out."

A glass-topped bar sliced off a third of the room. Behind it a corn-haired girl was watching them. Overdeveloped breasts bulged from a slubbed silk sheath. The wall behind her was decorated with a photo-montage representing a public execution. The scene had obviously been blown up from an old daguerreotype. A tophatted hangman posed on the scaffold, one hand displaying the noose, the other thrust into the recesses of his frock coat. His blindfolded victim wore a collarless shirt and had his arms pinioned behind his back. The whiskers on the faces of the onlookers dated the occasion. The other walls were decked out with texts done in Gothic lettering:

Repent — for the kingdom of heaven is at hand
The wages of sin is death
He is everywhere

There was a recruiting poster for the police force — a helmeted cop smiling and beckoning at the club members. These milled about the tables and bar, indifferent to the décor.

The man put the glass of tomato juice down very carefully. He was built like a fast middleweight in training. He jerked his head.

"I said 'out.' Try further down the street. Knock twice and ask for Nelly. And give us a miss on your way back."

Thorne spoke no louder than he had to. "I was told to ask for Mr. Chalice. Kosky sent me."

The man switched his appraisal to Cameron. What he saw made no visible impression.

"What do *you* do?" he asked. "Dance?"

Cameron's face darkened. But his voice was controlled. "Kosky sent me too."

A girl in a red wig and with a skirt a foot above her knees started screaming that she had been insulted. Her escort laid a heavy hand across her mouth and continued his conversation without looking at her. A broad-shouldered man sitting in front of them came to his feet. He moved with deceptive laziness. He wore a well-tailored gray suit, black brogues and a silk knitted tie. He ruffled his hair as if to make sure that it was all there. His smile came and went.

"My name's Chalice. Sit down."

The younger man sat with them, morose and watchful. Chalice jerked his head at him.

"Crying Eddie. He's not in very good form today. He can't make up his mind whether someone went down his trousers while he was in kip last night. That sort of thing upsets him. That and buying a drink."

Crying Eddie fixed a cold eye on his partner. "The only thing upsets me, mate, is you making a bleeding fool of yourself."

Chalice's grin widened showing teeth in good repair. "I talked to Kosky on the blower. Anyone he sends is welcome. See if you can get Doll away from those swells at the bar, Ed, and get us a drink. Champagne, Scotch, tequila. You name it we got it," he said jovially.

Thorne's thin mouth set nervously. It was the sort of rat trap he had always avoided — patronized by people on temporary leave of absence from jails up and down the country. Con men who looked like judges, showgirls masquerading as debs, bookmakers looking like bookmakers.

Crying Eddie used his shoulders to force his way through the crowd round the bar. Chalice's face sobered. "Don't worry about Eddie and don't be took on by them leather trousers. He'll have a go at anyone. He don't drink and he don't smoke and birds cost money."

Thorne felt Cameron's foot on his ankle. He cleared his throat.

"Did Kosky tell you what we wanted?"

A tall man with a bald head and bent nose waved across the room. Chalice returned the salute genially.

"Icepick Willie. Strike a light anywhere near him and he'll go up in flames. Of course he told me what you wanted. We're glad to oblige."

Thorne sensed that Chalice's casual manner wasn't going down well with Cameron. He tried for something more positive.

"It's a doctor we came for, not a drink. We've got someone in a flat in Chelsea, badly burned."

Chalice produced a thin cigar. He wore rather than smoked it, rolling it unlit from one side of his mouth to the other.

"I know," he said mildly, "but I *offered* you a drink."

Crying Eddie weaved through the crowd, carrying the glasses high over his head. He put them down on the table and swung his leg over the back of his chair. Chalice took the cigar from his lips.

"We better get this straight. Kosky don't give me no orders. He does me a favor — I do one for him. Give and take, like. But I want to know a little more about this sort of lark than I do now. Is Old Bill on your tail?"

Thorne sought the faded freckles on his nose. "Old Bill?"

"The law," Chalice said amiably.

Cameron's face was hard. "There must be something wrong with your hearing. Or maybe you didn't understand what he said. A man's badly hurt. What do you want — his fingerprints?"

The hush at the table was accentuated by the loudness of the surrounding voices. Crying Eddie's chair scraped back a couple of inches. His relaxed pose promised explosion.

"It's Danyerl Boom," he said acidly. "That's who it is."

"Belt up." Chalice's shrewd eyes searched the Canadian's face. "Who are you, mate — where'd you come from?"

This time it was Thorne who tried to reach Cameron's foot under the table. The Canadian ignored the warning, matching Chalice's scrutiny as if the issue were important.

"Bruce Cameron's my name. You don't need my life history. All we want to know is whether or not you're going to help."

A thin scar clipped the side of Chalice's swarthy cheek. He massaged it thoughtfully.

"I never heard of either of you." He managed to make it sound a logical reason for his attitude. "But I've already told you I'm going to help. Now drink your drinks."

What was happening was against Thorne's habits and training. The smoke cloud he'd created over the years was being dispersed. The feeling was strong that something had sparked between Chalice and Cameron — it was as if a distress signal had been flashed and answered. He did what he could to identify himself with it.

"We'll make it worth your while, naturally."

Chalice laid the chewed cigar in the ashtray. "Naturally. Get the car Ed. Wait on the corner of Trebeck Street. I'll be out as soon as I've changed me shoes."

His partner got up slowly, flexing his shoulders, strengthening the image of a good, fast middleweight.

"Do you want to know what I smell, mate. Trouble. And don't say I didn't warn you. You and your bleeding Kosky."

Chalice grinned as the blond man walked away. "That don't mean anything. He just likes the sound of his own voice." He rose to his feet.

The group shooting poker dice at the next table looked up as he neared them. He stopped and took the leather cup from the man who was holding it. His voice had a starchy friendliness.

"Howdyer feel tonight, Biff — lucky?"

The man had bright button eyes set in a tight face. He smiled back as if it cost him money.

"With you I always feel lucky."

Chalice's dark face grew pensive. He held the cup close to his ear, rattling it.

"Some people in this place think you're a trouble-maker, Biff, did you know that?"

The circle fell silent. Heads were studiously turned. The stiff poses warned of tension. The man lifted his shoulders.

"How about you, Harry. What do *you* think?"

Chalice lowered the cup. He shot the dice, leaving a pair of aces. The third throw showed a full house, aces high. He turned the cup upside down on the table.

"I think they're right. Get out of here, Biff, and don't come back. And remember to pay your bill before you go."

He removed the man's clenched fingers from the edge of the table as if the sight offended him. The man stood, white faced and shaking.

"Do you know something, Harry. It's the first time I've ever been barred by one of my own. I'll be seeing you."

Chalice allowed a brief glimpse of his teeth. "Any time, any place, Biff. And Eddie does the worrying for me. Goodnight, mate."

He stayed close to them as far as the bar. The man threw a bill on the counter and left without waiting for the change. Thorne raised his eyes. Chalice was going through a door on the far side of the room. He and Cameron were the only ones watching him. Otherwise the scene had played itself out in front of a blasé audience. Thorne did his best to sound equally at ease.

"Kosky said he's reliable."

Cameron stubbed out his butt. "One thing's sure —he's not likely to wet himself when the pressure's on."

Chalice reappeared, coming through the crowd like a politician in friendly territory. He smiled, winked and nodded his way to their table. He'd collected his overcoat lined with fur. The shoes he'd changed into were sturdier than the elegant brogues — black and with soles a little too thick for fashion.

"Let's be off, then." He made it sound like an invitation to a football match.

As Thorne passed, the girl in the red wig grabbed his arm, her voice whiskey-shrill. He removed her hand under the glare of her thick-eared admirer. Chalice made room for his elbows at the expense of the nearest drinks on the bar. He leaned across, smiling at the blonde.

"I'm going out for a bit, Doll. Don't serve no drinks after time and try to keep the High Society from breaking the furniture."

She twisted the solitaire on her finger, her face sulky under a layer of Max Factor pancake.

"You're *always* going out."

He nodded pleasantly. "I'm a popular man. Mind how you go."

She made a face as he turned away. They followed his confident saunter from the room. He closed the door, put an ear against the panel and listened for a moment. He straightened up, speaking to no one in particular.

"Eleven thousand quid this dump stands me in, believe it or not. She kept on at me best part of a year. 'Buy me a place in Mayfair, Harry. *That's* where I want to be — that's where I *belong*.' Look at the joint! Look at the people! One blast on a copper's flute and they'd all be diving through the window. 'Highclass,' she said. Gawdalmighty! OK. It's a black E-type CIX 500. Don't get too close up behind and remember to give yer eyes a chance."

The Jaguar's taillamps snaked into the park. Vapor formed round the dual exhausts, blueing the chilly air. Cameron kept the station wagon a couple of lengths in the rear, driving in complete silence.

North of Bayswater Road the Jaguar turned into a street angling Inverness Terrace and stopped. Cameron stopped on the opposite corner. They watched Crying Eddie leave the Jaguar and run up the steps of a small house. He rang the doorbell. The hall light came on immediately. The door was opened quickly and Crying Eddie disappeared inside.

Cameron lit a fresh butt, sitting humpbacked as he watched the house. Thorne eased his legs surreptitiously.

"Someone'll have to do something about Robin's mother."

Cameron stirred out of his slump. "That's about the tenth time you've said it. What do you suggest we tell her?"

"The sort of thing she'd want to believe. That Robin's gone to Paris with this girl Sandra Jellicoe. She's rich and a ward-in-chancery so Robin's lying low. The old bag'll be delighted."

Cameron took the cigarette from his mouth. "From everything I remember, she couldn't care less. He spent more time away from home than in it. Why should she suddenly flip if she doesn't see him for a night?"

A couple of queers minced by, gray faced and hungry eyed. Thorne looked at the dash clock. It was getting on for ten. In a few hours they'd be reading his letter at Scotland Yard. It wasn't difficult to sound anxious.

"Why? Because she's his mother for a start. Don't

push this commanding-officer bit too far. At least I know what *should* be done and seeing Mrs. Gunn is part of it. We seem to have dispensed with logic since you took over. Pistols — racing about London with a couple of thugs. All because you developed a conscience. Have you asked yourself how far Robin would have gone for you?"

Cameron looked at him oddly. "Strangely enough I haven't. What's worrying you so suddenly, anyway. The police don't know who they're looking for."

Thorne felt as though he was moving towards the edge. "I know. But they'll have a working theory of what happened at Palaton's by tomorrow morning. It didn't matter before. With Robin in your flat it does. All it needs is someone like that girl — the one you spoke to outside your house — a nosy milkman or landlord — *anyone*, for Chrissakes. Anyone who senses there's something funny going on in your place — that you're trying to hide something — and you have a caller from Chelsea Police Station."

Cameron shrugged. "You're chasing your tail. We'll be out of the place in an hour and we'll take Robin with us. Chalice'll have to get us another car."

He broke off as the door of the house opposite opened. Crying Eddie appeared, leading a man in dark glasses. The man tapped his way down the steps with a white cane. Cameron's incredulity hardened to accusation. The Jaguar had turned round. It faced them, headlamps blinking.

"They want us to follow," Thorne said hurriedly.

The southbound traffic was hard to penetrate. Souped-up minicars scooted around the loaded buses —cabs bluffed their way out of side streets. Christmas lights still blazed in the shop windows. A red-hooded Santa in Kensington was peddling gifts from the North Pole at a shilling a throw. Chalice's face showed at the back of the Jaguar. He waved Cameron on. The station wagon shot ahead, beat the King's Road signals and gunned down Oakley Street. He pulled up outside his flat. The Jaguar passed and stopped a hundred yards away. Cameron killed the motor.

"See them in."

He ran down the steps. Thorne watched the approaching trio with apprehension. The blind man was in the middle. Crying Eddie carried his cane; Chalice, a Gladstone bag. Thorne bolted the door behind them. Cameron was already in the bedroom. Thorne pointed the way. They filed into the stuffy room and stood round the bed. As far as Thorne could see, Gunn had not stirred. Chalice went straight to the window and lifted a corner of the curtain.

"OK, Ed," he said shortly.

His partner removed the doctor's hat and glasses. Only then did Thorne realize that the man's eyes were covered with adhesive tape. Eddie whipped the strips off. The doctor stood there blinking. He was old and shabby with the sallow skin of a Hindu who has been too long out of the sun.

He leaned down over Gunn, a stethoscope dangling

from his neck. He lifted one of Gunn's eyelids. His reaction was immediate. He grabbed at his instrument bag and fitted a needle to a syringe. He pushed the needle into the neck of a phial, bared Gunn's thigh and sank the plunger. Then he plugged the stethoscope in his ears and sounded Gunn's heart. He stepped away from the bed, a yellow man in a suit too large for him. His voice was a singsong of finality.

"This man is dead."

The hammer in Thorne's chest grew loud. His first impulse was to unlock the street door and start running. It didn't matter where as long as he removed himself from the scene. Cameron was standing against the dressing table, his face a mask of disbelief. He hooked a hand round the doctor's wrist. His voice was harsh.

"You don't know what you're talking about — he's drunk, not dead."

Crying Eddie's face was as impassive as his partner's. The doctor's eyes were monkey-sad. He spoke submissively.

"I am sorry."

He began repacking his instrument bag. Chalice looked round the room as though committing the scene to memory. He touched the doctor on the back.

"Come on, Alex." He turned to Cameron. "So long, mate."

The Canadian vaulted the dead man's body and stood blocking the doorway. The gun in his hand was pointing directly at Chalice's stomach.

"You're not going anywhere."

The quickness of his move had taken everyone by surprise.

Chalice's eyes were wary but unafraid. It was Crying Eddie who broke the spell, bringing his hand up very slowly, palm uppermost. He looked at it as though it belonged to a stranger and shrugged.

"I said it was Danyerl Boom, didn't I?"

The Canadian shifted the gun in his direction. Crying Eddie pantomimed an insult with pursed lips. Cameron spoke to Chalice. "I may be a mug but I'm not *that* sort of a mug. This thing's loaded. Your pals can go. You're staying."

Chalice shrugged. Cameron stepped away from the doorway, indicating the blond man. "Tell him to get this quack out of here and come back later."

Chalice's hands pantomimed despair like a Jewish comedian. "You heard him, Ed."

The Hindu waited patiently while Crying Eddie thumbed the plaster strips back across his eyes. He adjusted the dark glasses. Thorne let the pair out through the street door. He stood there for a moment, listening to the cane tapping along the railings. Seconds later came the low rumble of the Jaguar. He went back to the bedroom. Someone had draped a blanket over Gunn's body. The shrouded figure separated the two men.

Cameron set himself, speaking right at Chalice. "I'll put it on the line — the guy on the bed just earned himself the part of twenty thousand quid. Do you want it?"

Chalice's cufflinks were made of gold nuggets. He

examined them with care. The sight seemed to remind him of something he felt obliged to put to the others.

"I'll tell you. Me and Eddie's been thieves since we were kids. Nobody minds a bit of porridge. But we don't neither of us want to finish up in the topping shed."

Cameron jerked his. "What's hanging got to do with it? That guy committed suicide with a can of gasoline. Because he was always just that much smarter than anyone else. While he was alive I did everything I could for him. Now he's dead he means just one thing to me. Ten years in jail. I want to buy my way out of it. You're a pro — tell me how."

Chalice's eyes were fixed on his shoes. He lifted his gaze speculatively.

"What are you going to do — if I get up and start walking?"

In that moment Cameron was the grim stranger standing at the bar in a Western movie.

"Why don't we find out?" he said simply.

"I ain't going nowhere," Chalice said hastily. He explored a cavity with a broken match.

Cameron's hand took in the whole of the drab apartment. "Look at it! the sum total of thirty-six years endeavor — up till tonight. Now everything's different. I've got more money than I ever had at one time in my life. I'm going to keep it. Gunn's dead. I want him buried so deep that he'll never come back — not even for his mother."

The phone rang before Chalice could answer. Cameron grabbed at the receiver.

"What number do you want?" he asked in a voice that was not his own.

A woman's voice sounded hollowly. Cameron clapped his hand over the mouthpiece.

"It's Jamie. She wants to know if you're here."

Cameron shoved the receiver into Thorne's hand. He spoke as normally as he could manage. He heard her gasp of relief.

"I'm sorry. It couldn't be helped, Jamie. I was just going to phone you. Something's happened — I can't explain on the phone. We're going down to the country. I don't *know* when — in a couple of hours — an hour — I can't be sure. Just pack a bag and wait."

Her voice was distraught. *"What's* happened? Henry, don't *do* this to me — are you in trouble?"

He smiled from habit, the understanding smile he reserved for her.

"Just pack the bag, Jamie. I'll explain everything later. Don't worry." He hung up and shrugged at Chalice. "My wife. Lying's not my strong suit."

"You get by," said Cameron. He walked round the bed and thumbed Jamie's picture out of the mirror. He ripped it across twice and threw the pieces in the trashbasket. "You get by," he repeated.

Chalice's stare was suddenly shrewd and assessing. Thorne matched it with what he hoped was a look of sincerity.

The heat in the small room was stifling. The lights from the bedside lamp slanted across the blanketed body, deepening the lines in Cameron's face. He watched Thorne broodingly. The gun in his hand was only inches from Chalice's head. The dark man shifted his legs cautiously.

"The laws been having a go at me for six years. I've been picked up coming from a wedding — taking the dog for a walk. They even done me once coming out of my lawyer's office. Three times in six years they've had me inside and three times I beat them. Do you know why?"

"Personality," said Cameron. "You reek of it."

Chalice pushed the barrel of the gun away from his ear. "When you're inside you *get* no friends. It's because every time I take a chance I think ahead. You aren't giving me the chance."

Cameron hesitated. Then he thrust the gun into his pocket. "All right," he said heavily. "Beat it. Get the hell out of here."

Thorne looked stonily at the bed. Gunn's feet peeped from the end of the blanket. Everything Chalice had said reinforced his own forebodings. For the first time he began to realize the degree of danger inherent in Cameron. It wasn't Jamie or the money — these were only of relative importance to the Canadian. Deep down, only one thing mattered to him — a hatred of Henry Thorne that was so great that he was ready to destroy himself with its object.

Chalice made no move to go, lolling with one eye half shut. "My trouble is I'm greedy," he volunteered. "Twenty grand's a lot of money. But then so's a fiver if you haven't got it. How'm I supposed to know it's there?"

Cameron's manner was terse. "You could try a crystal ball. Or take my word for it. I can't show you the money here and now if that's what you mean."

Chalice went into a cloud. He came out of it, wearing an expression of interest.

"What's all this about going to the country? Where, for instance?"

Cameron spoke bleakly. "Tell him."

The outcome was already decided. The taut lines in Cameron's face — Chalice's perverse switch of ground proved it.

"It's a farmhouse," Thorne said carefully. "In the middle of nowhere."

Chalice stretched out his legs, looking at his sturdy shoes. "All right, mate. You bought yourself some help." He made it plain that he had accepted Cameron as spokesman.

Cameron took a deep breath. "You'll be paid. You've got my word for it." He pulled a drawer open, took out a passport and some papers. He threw these and a few clothes into a bag.

He stood by the bed for a moment gazing down at the body under the blanket. He walked over, stiff legged, to where Thorne was sitting.

"I just could be wrong about you. I'm going to make sure. Let's see what you've got in your pockets."

The muscles tightened in Thorne's chest. He managed to meet Cameron's pale-eyed stare. Cameron's grin involved no more than a bare widening of his mouth. He turned his pockets inside out, holding the gun with a finger thrust through the trigger guard.

"That's the lot, Henry. Don't disappoint me."

Thorne's hand crept into his clothing. His outstretched palm offered his collection. Some coins, a five-pound note, a pipe cleaner. He added the three keys. His head came forward.

"I found these on the floor of the car. They must have dropped out of Robin's clothes."

Cameron lifted the keys from Thorne's palm. "Well — imagine that," he said slowly. "I wonder why?"

Thorne set himself. "Because keys get lost. Or is that too fanciful for you?"

Cameron's voice was clipped. "No. No, it's not too fanciful, Henry. I'm wondering why I never knew about it before."

Something in the other's eyes told Thorne to tread warily. "I always understood you *did* know, Robin did. He was supposed to dump these with the others."

Cameron smiled insultingly. "No good at lying? You're a genius, Henry. A lot of things are starting to add up in my mind. From now on you're staying where I can get my hands on you. Stand up!"

He did as he was told, the look on his face that of a man fighting something too big for him — something unjust.

"Have it your own way, Bruce," he said.

Cameron's hand encouraged Thorne to the door. "I will."

He led the way along the passage and threw open the sitting room door. He glanced at the barred window.

"It's a good place to think, Henry. Especially when time's running out."

The door slammed and the key was turned from outside. Cameron's footsteps retreated along the passage.

BRUCE CAMERON
22nd December

SOMEONE was coming down the basement steps. Fingers rattled on the front door. Three soft knocks followed. Chalice relaxed.

"That's Eddie."

Cameron unbolted the door. The blond bulled by without a word. Cameron's fists clenched, but he kept a grip on himself. Chalice was waiting for them, his feet up on the end of the bed. He shielded his eyes with his hand, peering at his partner.

"You awake, Ed?"

Crying Eddie snorted. "I've got some news for you, mate. Next time one of your good friends needs a doctor leave Alex out of it. He doesn't want to know any more."

Chalice took his feet down. "That's show business. Never mind. We're going down to the country. A little job of work."

Crying Eddie's mouth sagged. He looked at the bed with disbelief. Chalice nodded.

"Twenty grand."

His partner's glare was belligerent. "You ought to

be branded a nut case. Alex wasn't kidding. The geezer's dead."

Chalice nodded comfortably. "Then he won't worry where he's buried, will he?"

Crying Eddie's voice broke. "Now I *know* you're not safe! What do you mean, the *country?*" The idea seemed to obsess him.

Chalice's face was serious. "You know what country is. Fields and that. Fresh air."

The blond sounded close to tears. "What's fields got to do with it? Have you got any idea when Christmas is — in three days' time! I've got fifteen relations coming to my house. What do you think they'll be doing while I'm not there — nicking everything that's not nailed down. And what about my old lady?"

Chalice was uncooperative. "What about her? Anyone who can nick anything out of the house with your ma around deserves a medal. What you getting in a state about, anyway. Nobody said anything about you having to milk cows. All you got to do is drive us there."

Crying Eddie shifted his weight without appearing to move his body. He looked full at Cameron, making no secret of his hostility.

"I never thought I'd live to see the day. What you going to move him in — a hearse?"

Chalice shook his head slowly. "Your sense of humor ain't that good, mate. It's all that vegetarian gear you eat — it rots your brains. Shuddup and lissen. Sam Rabin's got an old Humber on his lot — black with a big pullman body. If he's not at the dogs he'll be home. Anyway Anna'll be there. Bid them a two and a half for it. And see if you can get hold of one of them cabin trunks — try Jack Gellert. Make sure there are no markings on it. As soon as you've performed give us a ring here."

Crying Eddie put his hands over his small flat ears as though he wanted to block out all sound. Suddenly he picked up the phone. For a moment it looked as though he was going to hurl it at the wall. He put it down and scribbled the telephone number on a piece of paper. He gave one last despairing look round the room and walked down the passage. The door slammed behind him.

Chalice lounged over to the bed and pulled the blanket back. The body appeared to have shrunk. Brownish spittle had leaked from the mouth onto the pillow. The open eyes were swiveled sideways. Chalice dropped the blanket.

"Are you going to take that pistol with you?"

Cameron snapped his lighter. The gesture was becoming monotonous. A few drags — a stubbed cigarette — another smoke. He had an instinctive respect for the other man and wanted him to understand.

"I don't have any choice."

Chalice shook his head. "Why not? Eddie and me ain't slags. You don't need no pistol for us, mate. Who is it you're worried about — the Professor?"

Cigarette smoke drifted in front of Cameron's eyes as he sought the answer. Thorne's thin face looked into his consciousness. He tapped the cigarette ash onto the floor. "That's right, the Professor."

Chalice's smile was a blend of humor and cunning. "Then do me a favor — don't blow no holes in him while I'm here. One's enough."

Thirst drove Cameron to the kitchen. He drew himself a glass of water and sipped it, looking round the kitchen. His eye caught the earthenware pot that Jamie had painted. Most of the things that reminded him of her were gone. Smashed — given away or thrown out with the garbage. His gaze settled on the oven. Something niggled his memory. The open oven door — that was it. Vaguely he remembered closing it. But why would it be open? The oven hadn't been used since Jamie had left him. He went over and lifted the heavy metal handle. It was impossible for the door to *fall* open. The oven was empty. Suddenly he remembered something else — Thorne at the sink, blinking as the lights came on. In that minute he knew that Henry had opened the door. What he didn't know was *why*.

He went back to the bedroom. Chalice was in front of the mirror using his fingers as a comb. He swung round, his teeth a slash of white in his dark face.

"Wait till you hear this, mate. Where do they keep money — answer, in a bank. Coffee goes in a coffeepot. So what happens to dead bodies — you put them in graves. Get it?"

Cameron shook his head wearily. "No."

Chalice blocked a yawn. "Or one of them big

vaults. They prolly got a load of 'em in the country."

A possibility lurked behind the ghoulish humor. It just could be. He imagined a deserted village, the youngsters dispersed to the nearest towns, a vicar who preached to an empty parish church. Outside under mildewed yew trees would be forgotten headstones, graves long since untended. If the digging were done carefully and the turf properly replaced, Robin's burial wouldn't leave a trace. Winter and the spring rains would finish the job.

Chalice made one of his sudden mental jumps, going into a sort of Elder Statesman pose.

"Lissen, mate. I want to talk to you. Sit down."

Cameron took a chair. The window had been opened. The curtains billowed in the wind. A slit of light under the sitting room door speared the darkened passage. Chalice put his question point-blank.

"How'd you get lumbered into this lark — you don't look like a villain and you don't act like one."

Cameron balled his shoulders. "I had an unhappy childhood. So I was sitting outside this café drinking Pernod when this girl came up — a real witch. She said, 'why don't you give up, Bruce. The hell with this struggle for recognition. Just take their money.' As I say, a real witch."

Chalice's frown deepened. "That's a blinder, mate — a blinder! All right, let me put it this way. I don't know anything *but* thieving; I never asked myself whether it's right or wrong — but you do. That's why you're going to wind up in dead trouble."

Cameron used his lighter three times on yet another cigarette. "Twenty thousand pounds take care of most trouble I ever heard of."

Chalice made room on the end of the bed. His hand was only inches away from the splayed feet.

"That's what *you* think. It won't get you out of the trouble *you're* heading for. You and the Professor's after the same bird, right?"

It was a fair question in Chalice's world — the rough, puzzled earnestness made it clear. Perhaps twice in a year he'd talked about Jamie. Propped in front of some bar, listening to a jukebox play the remembered tunes. A kitsch production with a bored barman coming in strong with yes and no at the appropriate times. He sensed that this man *wanted* to understand. Maybe he wouldn't approve, but at least he wanted to help. The trouble was how to answer him.

"Once," he said truthfully.

Chalice moved Gunn's feet a fraction. "It sticks out a mile, mate. Not that it's any of my business. But I'll tell you something for your own good. The Professor's a dodgy bastard. Kosky says he's solid, but Kosky's dodgy too. I just keep ahead of him. All them Poles say that he gave up his own brother to get out of Warsaw. I can *smell* a slag, Canada. And that's what the Professor is. Watch him."

Cameron lifted a shoulder. "That's what I'm doing. I'll tell *you* something, too. I'm watching our money — yours and mine."

Chalice brought the tips of his shoes together, considering them thoughtfully.

"That's right, mate. Don't forget the money. Like that bird told you, it's the money that counts."

He lifted a grin that helped Cameron stumble into the confession that all along he'd sensed must come.

"What the hell. Why *shouldn't* you know. I hate their guts, the pair of them. I think of them the way you think of an old friend who suddenly lets you have it in the back. Three of us risked our liberty for this money. One's dead. I'm hostile, Chalice, but I'm not out to cut my own throat."

Chalice digested the statement thoroughly. "I've taken a fancy to you, mate, after a while. You ain't no weasel. Here — get a load of this."

He slipped his shoes off and laid them in his lap, soles uppermost. He produced a nailfile with the flourish of a conjurer and started scraping the heel of the left shoe with the edge of the file. There was a round leather plug in the center. He dug in the point of the file and pried the plug loose. It came out in his fingers. He showed Cameron the flanged screw underneath. A twist of his wrist and the heel lifted off. He did the same thing with two more plugs and half the sole came away. He repeated the performance with the other shoe and held both out to Cameron. He looked peculiarly pleased with himself.

The upper part of the soles was hollow. One contained a packet of hacksaw blades wrapped in oiled paper. In the other was what looked like a flick knife. The left heel held a wad of money, the right three handcuff keys. He fitted the shoes together again. His face had become wary.

"Nobody ever seen that before except Eddie. He's got a pair himself. Try 'em on."

He pushed the shoes at Cameron. They were a little big, but apart from that felt like any other shoes. Cameron gave them back. Chalice laced them on and straightened up, flushed with exertion.

"I'll get you a pair made. *And* I'll supply the fittings. These handcuff keys'll fit any pattern the law uses. A frame for the blades is easy. Knock the glass out of a cell mirror and you're in business. They'll take care of any bars *I* ever seen."

The last six hours spun in Cameron's mind with macabre persistence. Robin's screams as he ran in flames — the tapping cane of the Hindu doctor — the strange comradeship of the man sitting opposite. Superimposed on every picture was a thin foxy face wearing the faintest of smiles. He lifted his hand, not knowing how to express his gratitude. The phone rang in that moment. Cameron grabbed the receiver, listened briefly, then cradled it.

"Eddie. He's on his way over."

Chalice fiddled with the gray streak in his hair as if trying to measure its width.

"Lissen to me, Canada. I don't want to know your business. But I been at this lark a long time. I *know* the way Old Bill works. If the law hits this gaff, they'll go through it like a hot fly through butter. The Forensic Squad — ever hear of *them?* They'll take the floorboards up, the soap out of your razor — they'll even take the dandruff out of your hair. Then some pofaced bastard'll stand up in court and swear that the wind in your lungs came from the scene of the crime. You stand on me, mate. If they *want* you, they'll have you. Unless you *think*."

Cameron shook his head. "There won't *be* any cops here. They never heard of us. My rent's paid till March. I'm going to walk out of here tonight and keep going. When the landlord comes in he's welcome to what he finds. You don't want to know my business — OK. But I'll tell you this much. The guy on the bed's the only mistake we made."

Chalice wriggled his shoulders as if accepting the inevitable. He looked at the still form beside him. "A funny thing. It's the first one I ever seen. I've seen 'em carved up. Eddie's brother had a hundred and ten stitches put in him. But I never saw a dead one before. It makes you think. We better start moving him."

Cameron took a hold on Gunn's legs. The black silk socks had collapsed around blistered ankles. The combined stench of Scotch, burned fabric and flesh was nauseating. Strength bulged in the top half of Chalice's body as he took the strain. They carried their burden to the end of the passage and propped the body against the wall. It sagged with drooping head, unrecognizable as the boulevardier of a few hours ago. Someone tapped the sitting room door. Cameron swung round and threw it open. Thorne was standing as close as he could get to the exit. The skin on his cheeks looked as though it had been first stretched and then ironed. He pulled his hand up tight against his chest, pointing at the street.

"A car outside," he mouthed.

Chalice's hand flew to the light switch. He tip-toed to the window and looked up. A gate creaked. Someone ran lightly down the steps. The lights came on again. Chalice was looking at Thorne, his face sour. Cameron had a sudden urge to disassociate himself from his partner. He unbolted the street door. Crying Eddie's entrance left no doubt about the way he was feeling. He avoided the body in the passage, turning the corners of his mouth down. Snow was melting on his coat. He brushed more of it from his hair, flicking his wet hand with distaste.

"A nice quiet evening at Doll's, he says, and now look at me," he observed tragically. "Stand on me, you don't get me at this lark again."

Chalice shrugged into his fur-lined coat. "That ain't news. Did you get the motor?"

Crying Eddie looked round the room as if he expected the Murder Squad to appear from under the divan.

"I got it. But no cabin trunk. Jack Gellert's in 'The Prince of Wales,' pissed."

Chalice was indifferent. "Get on the blower, Canada. See what they say about the weather."

The bedroom stank of Gunn and stale cigarette smoke. He threw open a window, glad of the cold air on his face. He dialed ASK 6611. He'd lain on this very bed, Jamie in his arms, broke but at least a believer in something called happiness. Something positive. In just a few minutes he'd be walking out of the place for the last time, carrying a dead man. A few more hours and he'd have more money than he'd ever had in his life at one time. A premonition lurked at the back of every thought he had about the future. Telling himself it was no more than a guilt complex changed nothing. The weather report came through promptly. He went back to the sitting room.

"The roads are normal as far as Salisbury. A bit wet, that's all. After that they say there'll be ice patches. It's supposed to get worse as the temperature drops."

Chalice ignored his partner's soundless groan, rubbing the top of his head vigorously. He addressed himself to Thorne.

"Did you say your wife was coming with us?"

Cameron's nose wrinkled. It was all they needed. Thorne's forehead looked as though he'd washed and forgotten to dry it.

"That's what I said."

The affirmation seemed to stun Chalice. "Are you some kind of nut, mate? A load of villains with a stiff in the back of the car and you want your wife with?"

"I need her," Thorne said stonily.

Chalice's disgust lingered. "What do you say, Canada?"

He stared at them moodily. He was being put on show for a decision and resented it.

"What the hell do I care! Let her stay *or* go." It

was untrue. Deep down he wanted her as a witness of his triumph.

Chalice shook his head. "Nice people. Then somebody'll have to keep her quiet. It ain't going to be the time for hysterics."

Thorne picked the typewriter case from the table. "Can we take this, Bruce. I have my reasons."

The expression on his face was guileless and the whole thing done casually. It was the look in Thorne's eyes that warned Cameron.

"Reasons for what?"

Thorne seemed to be trying to convey a message. "I'll tell you later," he said finally.

Cameron's mind recreated the other's house — the drawing room desk — on top of it, the Swiss portable in its metal case. He took the machine from Thorne's hand and put it back on the table.

"You've *got* a typewriter."

Chalice said something to his partner in a low voice and left the room. They heard him run up the steps. Seconds later glass crashed in the street. A woman shrieked. The shriek became a wail. "Po-l-i—c—e!"

Crying Eddie burst out of the passage, swearing as he tripped over the body's feet. Cameron was close behind him. He climbed a few of the steps till his eyes came level with the sidewalk. The nearest street lamp had been shattered, leaving the parked car in darkness. Crying Eddie was already behind the wheel of the black Humber, motor running. Footsteps came pounding down the street. Cameron started back down into the basement. Chalice slid the last few yards, grabbing at the railings.

"Lively," he gasped. "Some old bird seen me do the lamp!"

As they went down the steps, Thorne tried to pass them, elbows flying. Cameron caught his arm, locked it behind his back and propelled him up to the sidewalk. He hurled him into the car.

"Watch him," he said to the driver.

Crying Eddie had donned gold-rimmed spectacles and a cloth cap. He swung round, a six-inch blade in his right hand.

"Move and I'll cut your heart out," he said to Thorne.

As Cameron reached the bottom of the steps, Chalice came through, Gunn's head rolling on his chest. He propped the body against the garbage can.

"I can do this on me own. You go up and get the trunk open. If you see anyone coming, put the block on."

Cameron scrambled back up. A bus turned the corner, barely slowing at the deserted halt. The faces of the upper deck passengers were blurred behind the fogged windows. He waited till the lights of the bus had gone. Chalice had hoisted Gunn in a fireman's lift.

"*Now!* said Cameron and broke for the back of the Humber. The trunk was unlocked, the key in it. He lifted the top as Chalice's head appeared out of the basement. Chalice trotted across the sidewalk and pitched his burden over his shoulder. Cameron dropped the top of the trunk and locked it. He climbed in beside Thorne. Chalice was sitting next to his partner. The car shot forward. Its lines were high and unfashionable, but the engine was responsive. Chalice coughed a couple of times, his breathing labored.

"Did anyone see which way that old bag went?"

The signals at the junction were red. Crying Eddie braked, watching the east-west traffic.

"To the nick, probably. What you did was real clever."

Chalice twisted the driving mirror, wiped his face and ran his fingers through his hair.

"It must be terrible to be born stupid. Nobody saw us load up, did they? And all *she* saw was me running. Which way do you want him to go?"

"Right," said Cameron. "Back along King's Road, then left by the Classic Cinema. Don't try to go in, it's a dead end."

Crying Eddie nursed the Humber into the mainstream of traffic. Chalice's breathing was easier.

"What about the numbers on this motor — did you ring 'em or not?"

The back of Eddie's head was rigid. "No, I didn't. And there's something else I didn't have time to do. Think up what I'm going to say when the Law stops us."

Chalice hunched as if answers were swarming in his brain. He came out of it, his voice bored but good humored.

"Your thinking's unhealthy, mate. I'm going to have to do something about it."

It was gone ten by the town hall clock. It had started to snow again, the thick flakes falling slantwise. A few patrons loitered under the canopy of the Gaumont Cinema, sheltering before returning to reality. Across the street a group of long-haired youths horseplayed with snowballs. Cameron lowered his window, beset by a sudden wave of doubt and claustrophobia. All his life he seemed to have been running from something. First the bleak Saskatchewan grain town, the dour manse from where his father relayed the news of God's love, Presbyterian style. From the wholehearted disapproval of a prairie university. From every lousy deal the Fate Sisters had offered him since. And he was sick of it. There seemed no place left to run to.

He lifted his head, meeting Chalice's ironical scrutiny. The car rolled, sending Thorne sprawling. Cameron shoved him away violently, loathing the bony wiriness of the other man's body. It was with *him* that Jamie slept nights, her flesh against his. Everything they'd done together in the name of love she did now out of what she called "respect." A whore, liar and hypocrite, yet so deep in his bones that words like "love" and "hate" were inadequate. He lit a cigarette, counting the number in the pack mechanically. He'd better get more before leaving civilization.

He no longer thought about Gunn. You died — someone buried you. But Thorne was alive. "No secrets from Henry," she'd said a million light years ago. How did she figure it? In any case, Henry had a couple of tiny secrets of his own. And his front was just about to go like a bottle in a shooting gallery.

Chalice sprawled in the front seat, a calculating eye watching the way ahead. He took the panatella from between his teeth, looking up at Cameron's reflection in the driving mirror. He winked deliberately. His untroubled grin inspired a feeling of comradeship that was all the stronger because of its sharply defined limits. He promised what he promised, fulfilled it and nothing more. Cameron's fingers closed on the butt of the gun in his pocket. If he did as much he'd do well. He leaned forward and tapped Crying Eddie's shoulder.

"Pull up here."

The driver eased the Humber to the curb. The entrance to the mews was thirty yards away. Edwardian street lamps lit the cobbled stretch between the small houses. Snow-shrouded cars were parked in front of doors that had been boldly painted in primary colors. There was an air of gaiety — of a hamlet of neighborly people. The fronts of the houses were bedecked with tubbed plants, picture windows. Here and there a perambulator was perched on the steps. Most of the curtains were flung wide showing rooms festooned with Christmas decorations. One of the houses was hung with a red-ribboned wreath.

Cameron opened the car door. "We'll be right back."

Chalice nodded. "Don't hang about. Eddie's nose starts running."

Thorne stepped out, the hood over his head. Cameron walked on his right, his hand deep in his overcoat pocket. More than anything in the world, he wanted to shoot Thorne squarely between the eyes.

JAMESON THORNE
22nd December

S HE SAT IN DARKNESS, listening to the racket coming from the Jensens' party. Every light in the house was ablaze. People had been coming and going for hours. Her sense of time had dulled since she had spoken to Henry on the telephone. Suddenly her ears picked up the sound of approaching footsteps. She ran to the window, knocking into the furniture in her haste.

Two men came into view, using the parked cars as cover as they hurried past the shouts and laughter. She had the street door open long before they reached the house. She shut it behind them and switched on the hall light. Thorne took the hood off his head slowly. She hid her face against his coat, clutching him tight. His body was tense and unresponsive. She lifted her head. Cameron was standing behind Thorne, his mouth sullen with hostility. She tugged at her husband's arms.

"For God's sake *say* something. What *is* it — what's happened?"

He disengaged himself, pushing by into the hall without answering. He collected a case of fly rods and laid them on top of the bag she had packed. He went into the drawing room. Cameron followed, planting himself in front of the dead fire as if he owned the place. She glanced into the mirror, nervous under their joint inspection. She rebuckled the sweep of blond hair. Thorne's appraisal was thorough, taking in her polo-necked sweater and stretch trousers, the fur-lined boots. His eyes held hers as if he meant them to say more than his mouth could — or *dare* — she thought with sudden intuition. The impression that he was desperately afraid was so strong that she held out her hand, wanting him to take it. He spoke in a voice that she didn't recognize.

"Get your sheepskin coat, Jamie."

Cameron lowered himself onto the arm of the sofa. He flicked an inch of ash onto the carpet. He looked at her for at least thirty seconds, smiling slightly as if the scene amused him. He released two thin streams of smoke from his nostrils and crossed his legs.

"Tell her, Henry, or do you want me to do it?"

A door across the mews slammed on a noisy farewell. She looked from one to the other, her voice unsteady.

"If you don't stop it, I'll burst into tears."

Cameron continued to smile. Her husband came towards her and took her cheeks in cold hands.

"Robin's dead."

Her fingers flew to her mouth. An image formed in her mind. An image of a crashed car, overturned, the wheels still spinning. And somewhere inside, Robin lying on his back. His face mocked her even in death. The whole thing was so real and vivid that she felt that she must have seen it happen.

"Oh no, I can't believe it," she whispered.

Thorne made sure that she did. "An accident. He was burned to death. We've got his body in a car round the corner."

Cameron dragged on his cigarette and released another dribble of smoke.

"What Henry means is that we've got Robin in the trunk where nobody will see him."

Fear beat in her heart and she started to shake. The implication was too horrible to accept. She did what she could to reject it. She went on shaking even when Thorne took her in his arms. He put his mouth against her ear.

"It's true, Jamie. I'm in serious trouble. I can't explain now but it's impossible to go to the police."

She looked up, seeing Cameron's remote smile through a blur of tears. She knew what it stood for instinctively. She broke free from Thorne's arms, clawing at Cameron's face and eyes.

"*You* did it — to destroy us! I hate you, do you hear me — *bastard!*"

He caught her flying hands by the wrists, increased the pressure till she whimpered with pain then let her go contemptuously. He picked his cigarette from the carpet. Thorne's arms imprisoned her.

"Listen to me, Jamie. Bruce isn't responsible — nobody's responsible. I told you it was an accident. *You'll* be the one who destroys us unless you get a grip on yourself."

"Destroy?" She repeated the word as if hearing it for the first time. She turned her back on Cameron and searched Thorne's eyes. She was suddenly and fiercely protective. She had never seen him like this, afraid and uncertain. And no matter what he said, she knew she was right. Bruce had trapped them both. He'd done what he'd sworn to do over a year ago. She sensed this was only the beginning. If she were to save them she had to fight as Bruce fought, mercilessly and with cunning. She shook her head.

"I'll be all right. I promise I'll be all right."

"I love you, Jamie," Thorne said quietly. "You know that, don't you?"

Her fingers twisted into his sleeve. "I know it and I'll never forget it."

Cameron's tongue lashed them both. "Remind me to narrow my bed. You're coming with us for one reason, Jamie. I like my enemies where I can see them. And the pair of you are going to behave yourselves or you'll just stop living." He drew his hand from his coat pocket and showed her the short-barreled pistol.

She looked deep into the pale blue eyes. Nothing showed but the outward edge of his hatred. She spoke through numbed lips.

"A man telephoned. He wouldn't leave a name but he asked for you."

Thorne gripped her elbows. "How long ago? What sort of voice was it?"

She tried to remember. "An hour — perhaps two — I don't know. But he was a German — foreign,

134

anyway. He said it had something to do with a stamp auction."

Cameron spoke sharply. "Call Robin's mother and let's get out of here."

The quick glance aside, the lifted chin and defiant glare — after all this time he couldn't deceive her. He was frightened himself. She lowered her eyes. Whatever she knew about him had to be kept secret now. Taped music from the Jensen house filled the mews, the Streisand voice belting out "Melancholy Baby."

"Go ahead and make the call," Cameron repeated.

Thorne picked up the phone and dialed. They heard the number ringing. There was no answer. Cameron's eyes narrowed.

"What number did you dial, Henry?"

Thorne told him. Cameron picked up the phone directory. She knew the mood only too well — rage-blind, aggressive and suspicious. He flicked through the pages, thumbed down under GU and spun the dial. He held the receiver at arm's length as if it were infected. He dropped it back on its rest after a couple of minutes and shrugged.

"Come on — let's go."

He opened the street door. She walked between the two men, Thorne carrying the suitcase and fly rods. She saw Margot Jensen through the window, hair piled on top of her head, the center of a voluble crowd. She had always despised everything the Jensens stood for, the with-it clothes and opinions, the preoccupation with worthless and superficial values.

Now she longed to be part of it — part of anything that would rescue her from the black evil bird that was enfolding her in its wings.

King's Road was frozen. The self-service store where she shopped was strung with lights. Paper-ruffed turkeys garnished with holly peeped from cold storage. Giant plum puddings stood under bunches of mistletoe. Goods canned from Hongkong to Vancouver were racked on the shelves.

They passed the Salvation Army choir singing carols outside the Markham Arms. A large black car was parked on the corner. Cameron pushed the Thornes into the back seat. His refusal to sit between them was derisive. Two strangers were already in the front. The driver wore a cap over ears set close to his head. Flat pale hair grew down his neck. The reflection watching her from the driving mirror had a sort of combative handsomeness. Eyes appraised her from behind gold-rimmed spectacles. The scent he used filled the car — sharp to the nose like limes. The man beside him swiveled broad shoulders, laying his arm along the top of the seat. His fingers were thick with beautifully manicured nails. An inch-thick streak of white divided his thatch of black hair. His voice rasped as if he either smoked a lot or drank.

"Relax, darling. There ain't nothing to be afraid of."

The light from the street pierced a slatted blind over the back window, patterning his swarthy face. She put her knees close together, pushing her hands deep in the pockets of the sheepskin coat. His look undressed her. She'd seen these faces before — in films, on television. Hard smiling masks that concealed a terrifying assumption of power. They belonged to a world reported by the sensational Sunday newspapers. GANG WARFARE HITS SOHO—VIOLENCE SPREADS IN LONDON'S UNDERWORLD. With fake exposés accompanied by long distance shots of groups sunning themselves on the Carlton beach, the faces carefully out of focus.

"You're going to be a good girl, aren't you?"

Words framed in her mind but her lips refused to utter them. Cameron answered for her.

"She'll be all right. Let's get going."

She found Thorne's fingers. He was sitting up very straight, his eyes fixed on the back of the driver's neck. She returned the pressure surreptitiously. As long as they stayed together, nothing mattered. She'd fight with him and for him. She leaned back as the car took off, blocking her mind against the thought of what lay behind her.

It was past eleven when she opened her eyes again. They were crossing Wimbledon Common. The headlamps picked out trees standing like scarecrows on the snowcapped turf. Lights from the complex of apartment buildings showed by the river. They dropped down a long slope where Victorian mansions lay lost in shaggy gardens, turned left and headed for the Guildford bypass.

The driver switched on the radio, drumming out the rhythm of the music on the wheel with his fingers. Nobody seemed to want to talk. She huddled in her coat, the shorn lining comforting her face. She was as close to Thorne as she could get — Cameron as far from her as possible. Most of the time, he stared out of the window. Once when she lifted Thorne's hand to her mouth, Cameron turned his head. His contempt was like a blast of cold air.

They were far into the Surrey hinterland with a ribbon of slush unreeling in front of them. The driver slowed as the road looped through the outskirts of a village. They crossed a church-square and a cluster of cottages. A stone boundary wall ran parallel with the highway. The verge was lined with chestnut trees. The car went into a skid without warning. She felt the brakes lock then the heavy vehicle slid across a patch of ice like a curling stone. The driver sat perfectly still, holding the wheel almost nonchalantly. Someone said "Jesus!" in a loud voice. The Humber glided on sedately till its nearside wheels jumped the grass. The car ploughed along the wall, tearing off door handles and stopped with a crunch of metal.

The two men in front scrambled out of the offside door and inspected the damage. The left fender was buckled and fouling the wheel. Chalice bent down, his neck thickening as he wrenched the fender free. Somewhere behind the wall, geese started gabbling. Chalice and his partner took their seats again. The car crawled back on the highway, only one headlamp working.

She heard the driver's voice for the first time. It had the same pessimism as his face.

"A nice quiet evening! Don't anybody laugh."

Chalice's finger jabbed at the windshield.

"Why don't you try to keep on the road — it's safer."

They were twenty miles beyond Basingstoke when the lights of a car showed, coming fast towards them. As it neared, she saw the box sign on the roof. POLICE. It flashed by, leaving an impression of heads turned in their direction, faceless but watchful.

The driver's hands tightened on the wheel. "This is where we get our collars felt for a certainty. If they ever let me out of the nick, Harry, remind me to sue you."

Chalice's bulk hung over the front seat. "Pull the blind up. See if you can clock 'em."

Cameron yanked the cord and peered back into the darkness. "They're turning round — they're coming after us."

Chalice took the news calmly. "Don't get your bowels in an uproar. Everybody gives his right name. The car belongs to you, Professor. You're taking us down to your house. I'm thinking of buying it."

He faced the front, stuck a thin cigar in his mouth and folded his arms. She opened her handbag and used a lipstick. It seemed perfectly natural—as though she was preparing for an important interview.

She watched Cameron take the gun from his pocket and hide it under the collapsed blind. The brassy clamor of an electric gong sounded behind them. Crying Eddie slackened speed gradually, his front right-hand wheel glued to the strip down the center of the

139

highway. The pursuing headlamps grew brighter till the Humber was trapped in their beam — a large black beetle scuttling for cover. The police car overtook, swung in sharply, forcing the Humber to the side.

There were three policemen in the car. One stayed at the radio phone on the dashboard. The other two walked back, stripping off their gauntlets in ominous fashion. They separated, flanking the Humber. And now she saw their faces. The one on the left had anchored his cap with a strap underneath his chin. Crying Eddie wound down his window. The cop poked his head into the car and gave them the benefit of a close scrutiny. She smiled nervously as his eyes met hers. He cleared his throat importantly.

"Whose car *is* this?"

It seemed a long time before Thorne answered. "It's mine."

The cop propped his forearms on the top of the window. "Have you got the logbook with you?"

Thorne nodded. Crying Eddie produced it from the glove compartment. The man studied the buff folder closely.

"And that's you, is it, Mr. Wallace Kearney?"

She was watching the second policeman from the corner of her eye. He had strolled to the back of the car and stood there with one foot on the fender. He tried the locked trunk. It could have been purely a reflex action. She realized that Cameron had seen him too. The Canadian's hand moved close to the hidden gun.

Thorne loosened his dufflecoat. "No, my name's Thorne. I bought the car only a few hours ago. There wasn't any time to change the registration." His pipe was an emblem of respectability.

The cop handed back the logbook. His breath reeked of cough lozenges.

"Can I see the insurance?"

She was the only one who noticed Cameron's hand creep under the blind and transfer the gun to his pocket.

Crying Eddie fished out a white slip and placed it on top of his driving license. There was a hint of boredom in his voice, as if he'd been doing this sort of thing for too long and had grown tired of it.

"The name and address are on the license. You don't want my birth certificate by any chance?"

The man's face reddened. She felt Cameron's body stiffen as the second cop passed the window. He leaned into the car. Someone had told him about the shrewd penetrating look, the voice of authority. He used both to the verge of caricature.

"Are these all friends of yours, miss?"

She touched Thorne's hand. "This is my husband. The other gentlemen are friends."

Chalice switched the dead cigar from one side of his mouth to the other.

"How long *that's* going to last Gawd only knows, you keep us sitting about here much longer."

The cop stamped the snow from his boots and lifted his chin. "We're doing this for the sake of our health — is that it?"

141

Suddenly she realized what was happening. The two men were deliberately baiting the police, drawing their attention from the back of the car. Chalice contented himself with a shrug.

"You're doing your duty, constable. We know that. All I'm saying is that it's cold with the winders down."

Cameron's hand moved beside her. She flinched, expecting to see the pistol. But he was offering her a cigarette. She held it in trembling lips, looking at the two policemen. The plea formed in her brain — *Help me!* — and then what? The lighter flared. Cameron's pale blue eyes warned as though he had read her thoughts.

The younger cop walked to the front of the car. He compared the details on the license plates with those on the tax sticker on the windshield. He came back, face thoughtful, running his hand along the gouged bodywork until he reached the window.

"You're driving with one headlight. You realize that's an offense, don't you?"

He waited for the admission. Whatever he planned to come next was knocked out of stride by Thorne's comments. Her husband's voice hardened noticeably.

"I think you're carrying this thing a bit too far. We're five responsible people trying to get between two points in particularly filthy weather. Our first piece of bad luck was to skid into a wall. You can see the damage it did to the car. What you can't see is the damage it did to my wife's nerves. My view is this — you'd be combining a sense of humanity with your duty if you tried helping us instead of treating us like a gang of criminals."

The outburst had an immediate effect. The cop's face registered misgiving. He withdrew his head smartly.

"Now wait a minute, sir. That's exactly what we *are* trying to do, *help*. The fact still remains that you've only got one headlamp working. That's a danger to yourselves as well as to others. Where are you supposed to be making for, exactly?"

"Templecombe," she heard her husband say.

The cop pulled on his gauntlets. "Then my advice is to have your lights seen to before you get there. There's an all-night petrol station about fifteen miles down the line. They might be able to do something for you. I'd certainly try. There's ice all over the place beyond Swindon and you look as if you'd had enough trouble for one night. Compliments of the season." He lifted his hand in salute and called his partner after him.

They sat in silence till the police car swept by in the opposite direction. One of the men in front was talking into the radiophone. The sound of their motor dwindled in the distance.

Outside, the night was without definition. Snow floated invisibly through the darkness putting a gag on everything it touched. Chalice wound his window up. The end of his cigar was mashed flat.

"Compliments of the season!" he said and blew hard.

His partner's face was sour. "There's no doubt about it, you're a comic, mate. And you know something else, you make me sick."

He switched on the ignition and rammed into low gear. They reached the gas station shortly after midnight, finding it in the middle of a small town smelling of fertilizer. It had a false front of rose-colored cement. A gray sports car behind a plate-glass window rotated on a stand, one full revolution to the minute. Staggered across the oil-stained tarmac were half a dozen gas pumps festooned with air lines and polishing rags. Crying Eddie touched the hornring. An elderly attendant appeared from a glass booth, incongruous in a uniform designed for a younger man. He looked at the broken headlamp, shaking his head defensively and scratching an armpit.

Crying Eddie poked his head from the window, scowling. "Watch your nut don't drop off, mate. You got a glass and bulb to fit this lamp?"

The old man assumed an ingratiating whine. "I'm only the night pump man, see. All the stores and that's locked up and Mr. Miller's got the key. There might be a bulb, though. I'll have a look."

Cameron called him back. "Where's the phone?"

The man's eyes were rheumy and tired. "That's locked up *too*. They've got one over at the caff." He pointed across the street. His voice held a permanent acceptance of injustice.

Four or five long-distance trucks were parked in front of a low building. A functional sign over the door said GEORGE'S PLACE — GOOD CHEAP EATS.

Cameron opened his door. The garish light deepened the lines round his mouth. He crooked his finger at her.

"Out — the pair of you."

Thorne nudged her. She picked up her handbag. Chalice climbed out, stretching and yawning. He went into a sort of jog that took him round to the other side of the car.

"See what you can do with the lamp, Ed. Won't be long."

His partner spat disgustedly through the window. Chalice led the way. Cameron walked between her and Thorne, his arms linked through theirs. Anyone watching would see no more than a friendly gesture but his muscles gripped like gyves, as if they were his prisoners. Her legs carried her forward automatically. Perhaps that's what they really were — prisoners. She saw their unknown destination as a dungeon where he'd keep them in misery till finally he killed them. Their feet crunched over frozen gravel, past the enormous trucks waiting like patient monsters. Chalice pushed the door of the café, enveloping them in a blast of hot air redolent of kerosene, stewed tea and fried bacon.

Cameron released her arm. She shook her hair loose, unbuttoning her sheepskin coat. A wolf-whistle came from a table on their right. Chalice swung round towards the sound. The deadpan faces at the table dissolved in smiles as he winked.

There was a formica-topped counter and behind it a fat man wearing a dirty T-shirt. What flesh was visible was covered with a matting of hair the color and texture of coconut fiber. His round bald head was sunk deep into beefy shoulders. Draped like a scarf round his neck was a dishcloth. He leaned both elbows on the counter, giving the impression that he neither refused nor courted custom.

Chalice nodded affably. "Five teas, mate."

The man counted heads and made four. He scratched behind his ear doubtfully.

"Five?"

"One to take." Chalice took the top off a glass case and prodded the pile of sandwiches.

The proprietor removed Chalice's hand and replaced the glass lid. He ran his words into one.

"Cheesehamliversausagebaconandtomato. They're all fresh. How many?"

Chalice was looking at his hand with mild surprise. "Five — ham."

Cameron pointed at the phone on the counter. "Can we use that?"

The man took aim with his dishcloth, surprising a fly on the wing. He draped the cloth round his neck again, breathing heavily.

"You give me the number — I get it."

"Western 0078," said Cameron. Neither the exchange nor number had any significance for her.

The proprietor hooked the phone to him with a fish fryer, saving his feet. He relayed the call to the operator and hung up.

"You got plenty time. You say you wanted mustard on them sandwiches or not?"

"Mustard," said Chalice. He pulled chairs for the four of them. An old cabinet radio was banging out pop music. The two kerosene stoves made the heat almost unbearable. She took off her coat. The men at the far table seemed to have lost all interest in them, arguing about loads and weather conditions. The counterman brought their food. She eyed it hungrily. It was nearly ten hours since she had eaten. The dark tea was honey-sweet and boiling, the ham packed in wedges of buttered bread. Chalice balanced a sandwich on the edge of a saucer and stood up.

"I'll take this out to the boy."

She shut her eyes, suddenly, feeling the salt burn of tears. It was all so horrible — a nightmare. Surely she'd wake in a minute, feeling the cat's claws striking through the bedcovers, Henry stirring beside her. She'd open her eyes on familiar shapes and be grateful for another day.

Cameron was sitting on the opposite side of the table. His smile was derisive.

"What's the matter with the pair of you — don't you like the company?"

She raised her head slowly, remembering another time and another voice. Recalling a promise of eternal friendship no matter what should happen between them. She tried to reach the man she once had known.

"Hate me if you like, but not Henry, Bruce. *I'm* the one who's responsible. All he's ever done is try to help you."

He pushed his food away as if he had suddenly tasted poison. He lit a cigarette, savoring the smoke before he answered. His voice was loud enough for them to hear — no more.

"You're a whore and a liar and a hypocrite. If I didn't find you slightly pathetic I'd despise you."

"I don't have to take that any more," she said angrily.

He shook his head at her, smiling again. "Oh but you do, sweetie, you do."

She stared at him stonily. The pity she had felt for him had been misplaced. *He* was the liar and hypocrite. Even the scene in her kitchen had been staged as part of his scheme to trick and terrorize till finally he achieved his revenge.

Thorne squared his shoulders as if expecting a blow. "It's not us you're destroying, Bruce — it's yourself. You seem to be losing everything — dignity, self-control — even your judgment."

Cameron grinned like a wolf. "Lucky girl — married to a man of dignity and perception instead of — what was it again — 'a psychopath'?"

The echo of her father's voice sounded in her ears. The faltering voice of a man who knows he has only hours to live. *Leave him, Jamie. He's no good for you. He's a psychopath who'll destroy you. Leave him before something dreadful happens.* All that had mattered then had been the surging violence of her emotion — the chemical excitement of just being with Bruce.

Thorne spoke doggedly. "Your *judgment*, Bruce! *You* know what's involved. What you think about Jamie and me doesn't matter one way or the other —

our safety does. Listen to reason. This call you've just booked will be child's play to trace. Don't you think this chap behind the counter will remember us? *Look* at him — look at us. They'll go across to the petrol station — get a description of the car and, for all we know, the number. And what about the police who stopped us?"

Cameron considered the ash on his cigarette, a skilled lawyer playing with a shifty witness.

"There's one bit of your argument I don't follow. Who's going to *want* to trace the call?"

Thorne leaned forward, gesturing nervously. "What about his mother? He's made a fool of her all his life. Suppose she doesn't believe this story about Paris and the Jellicoe girl. She phones the police and says her son's missing — tells them about a mysterious call she had from the country — after midnight. I'm not saying she *will* — I'm saying we can't afford to take the chance."

"What's the *real* reason, Henry?" Cameron asked shrewdly. "Why don't you want me to call her?"

Thorne wiped mustard from his mouth with the back of his hand. His voice sounded hopeless.

"All *right*. Let's have it your way. But when we're standing in the dock remember who's responsible."

She looked down at the table quickly, afraid that her eyes would betray her husband. She knew instinctively that he was acting a part. Cameron raised a hand, attracting the counterman's attention.

"Cancel that call to London!" He leaned his arms on the table. "Maybe I *did* lose my dignity. And my self-control. But *not* my sense of judgment. Mrs. Gunn's not going to worry because Robin's missing for a night. Maybe I'll have another idea. Meanwhile I get the message. You two think I'm really a good guy at heart. And you want to bury the hatchet — right between my shoulder blades!"

Nothing escaped her now. She recognized the doubt behind the Canadian's implacability — the agony of her husband's relief. "Here's Chalice," he said quickly. "There's no reason for him to know what we're talking about."

Chalice pushed through the door and deposited the cup and saucer on the counter. He came across and switched a chair under his rump.

"They've taped the glass back. It should hold. How much further we got to go, Professor?"

"About sixty miles," Thorne said.

Chalice turned his wrist, looking at the wafer-thin watch. His laugh started low down — he released it with gusto.

"I just thought of something. You know what my bird'll be doing now?"

His swarthy face was tilted back, mouth open, showing gold fillings. There was something feral about him that both fascinated and terrified her. She shook her head.

He wiped the corners of his eyes with a blue silk handkerchief.

"Lying in bed in curlers, reading *Queen* or one of them magazines. She's always dead sure they're going to have her picture. Know what, I give a geezer a fifty once — Major Collins, he called himself, said he was a journalist. He was going to get an article done about the club. Turned out to be a right con-man."

Cameron's cup clattered down on the table. "Let's get out of here for Crissakes."

She stood up, shrugging into the coat Thorne was holding for her. He spoke in a quick undertone.

"Careful, darling. They're dangerous, all of them."

The snowfall was thicker outside. They crossed the deserted street to the waiting car. The old attendant followed to the edge of the concrete canopy. The last she saw of him was a solitary figure standing, peering into the falling snow. The town dwindled to a cluster of lights linked to them by a lonely stretch of highway. A thick white coverlet was spread over the countryside. She dozed, on and off, wedged between Cameron and her husband. The few cars they passed were mostly in the outskirts of sleeping towns. Other than these, the only signs of life in fifty miles were the occasional flashing headlamps of friendly truck drivers. Crying Eddie had tuned the radio to a pirate station. The late night d.j. show blared on interminably, interspersed with fatuous attempts at humor. Suddenly an announcer broke in with a newscast.

". . . over the greater part of the country. Boxing Day racing has already been abandoned at Huntingdon and Newton Abbot. Stewards at both meetings made the decisions after inspecting the courses. Thieves broke into a plastics factory in the Isleworth area earlier today and stole sixty-one thousand pounds in cash. The thieves entered the strongroom with false keys, using a dummy laundry van to remove their booty. The van was found later in a sandpit fourteen miles away. An attempt had been made to destroy it with fire. The Trades Union Congress . . ."

Cameron's head jerked up. "Cut it off — cut the goddam thing off!" He reached across, pinning her back against the seat. The rest happened so suddenly. She saw her husband wince, Cameron's hand reaching for his face. She sank her teeth in the Canadian's wrist. He pulled it free. For a moment she thought he was going to strike her. Then Chalice swung round, catching hold of Cameron's sleeve.

"Easy, Canada," he said quietly.

Cameron shook himself out of the other's grip, looking at the teeth marks on his skin. He shrugged and went back in his corner. It was twenty minutes later when Thorne touched the driver's shoulder.

"There's a bridge coming up — a hundred yards round the next bend. Turn sharp left at the signpost and take it easy — there's a steep drop."

The Humber shot the bridge, rolling as the driver dropped down into middle gear and swung the car into the narrow lane. It crawled down the hill, shaving snow from the bolstered hedges. At the bottom of the hill, a thick wood encroached on the lane from both sides. Wind had acted like a snowplow, piling the drifts in v-formation. Beyond them was unrelieved darkness. They drove through the forest for twenty minutes then they were out of it. The snow swirled thicker, cutting visibility to twenty yards. She could just see the outline of a church, what must be a vicarage behind it. It was like coming into a ghost village. Half a dozen cottages huddled round a green and a frozen pond. There were no lights. No dogs barked. Nothing moved anywhere.

Thorne pointed to a lane behind the churchyard. A board at its end said PRIVATE — No THROUGH ROAD. "Up there."

The surface was white and unblemished. A mile on, the way was blocked by a gate set in post and rail fencing. Chalice dealt with it. They drove up a narrow avenue hemmed in by shrubbery. A house showed in the light of the headlamps. A two-storied building of brick and timber, square in the Queen Anne tradition. The car stopped. There was a path through the shrubbery to what looked like stables. A timber porch had been built on to the original back door. They stood under it as her husband groped under a bench. A match flared. Nothing surprised her any more — not even the key she saw in his hand. Something small and quick slithered through the undergrowth and plopped into nearby water.

The door was thrown open. Thorne thumbed a light switch. Cameron's eyes and mouth were sullen as he pushed her into the room. Rough unpolished pine had been used with imagination. The table and bench seats were made of it. The walls, floor and windows were all that remained of a stone-flagged kitchen. Thorne pulled curtains across the leaded panes. Beneath them was a gas stove, a sink and refrigerator. A deep-freeze unit was set against the end wall. A few pieces of pewter hung on a Welsh dresser. There was an earthenware pot filled with teazels in the middle of the dusty table.

She spread her coat on the bench and sat on it. There was a radiator behind her, another in the hall. Thorne lit a cigarette for her, his face pinched and wary. She tried to smile for him and failed miserably.

Crying Eddie was looking round the room as though he'd seen other places that he preferred. He looked even younger without his spectacles. He was wearing a camel's hair sweater underneath his car coat, thick-soled shoes and suede trousers. His fudge-colored hair was combed forward flatly — like an illustration in a Tudor missal. His elegance was almost effete, yet his face, she thought, had the menace and dedication of a storm trooper.

"It's here two o'clock in the morning," he said. "I'm going to be lucky to get home. Suppose somebody tells me what's happening." He said "somebody," but he was looking at Chalice.

Cameron walked over to the outside door and locked it. He faced them, holding the gun in front of him. She started to shake. It was when he was being dramatic that he was most dangerous. Action carried him to its own inevitable conclusion. He was impelled to violence and afraid of fear. Her hands started to tremble violently.

His voice revealed none of the things that she dreaded — it was quiet, reasonable and aimed at the blond man.

"*I'll* tell you what's happening. We're all after the same thing. Money. *I'm* the paymaster. The difference is that I've already earned my share. You're going to earn yours — all of you."

Crying Eddie leaned back against the deep-freeze. "You know what *I* think you are, mate," he said easily. "A big Charley — a mug. And you know what you can do with that thing you got in your hand — stuff it."

Chalice whipped in between them. "Belt up — the pair of you."

Suddenly she could bear it no longer. She broke into a fit of weeping, her head on the table. No one spoke. No one touched her. The weeping stopped as unexpectedly as it had begun, leaving a sense of utter helplessness. She looked up, feeling someone touch her shoulder. It was Chalice offering a glass of water. She took it gratefully, no longer afraid of him.

"Get her out of this," he told Thorne. "Get her up to bed."

Cameron had come a little closer. The gun was back in his pocket.

"She'll go when I say so. I want to see what there is upstairs first."

Crying Eddie laughed through his nose. His saunter was a direct challenge.

"Do *I* go or stay?" he asked his partner.

Chalice's swarthy face was impatient. "You stay till you're told to go. And you behave yourself. You got a motor here, Professor?"

Thorne shrugged. "A mini. The battery may be flat."

She sipped the water, understanding nothing of

what they were saying. Chalice perched on the end of the table.

"Who comes to this house — how'd you get your letters, f'rinstance?"

"A post van," said Thorne. "It makes the rounds of five villages. But I won't get any mail."

"What about the locals. Doesn't anybody keep an eye on the place?"

Thorne shook his head. "I don't shop in the district. There's always enough of what I want in the deep-freeze. I come and I go. Nobody pays any attention."

Cameron opened one of the two doors on the other side of the kitchen. She saw shelves stacked with cans, a potato sack. The Canadian unfastened the second door. Inside was an old-fashioned oil furnace, some pipes that must lead to an outside storage tank. Wood and coal was piled on the floor.

Chalice rubbed the back of his neck. "Light a fire and they know you're here, right?"

Thorne's thin face was superior. "There's a hill and six hundred acres of forest between here and the village. I've been here a week on end without seeing a soul. You might as well be in the middle of the Sahara."

She put the glass down, remembering the sudden journeys explained away as business trips. He must have got someone else to send the postcards that came from Milan, Hamburg, Paris.

Chalice said something to Cameron. It was too low

156

for her to hear but the Canadian shrugged. Chalice seemed resigned.

"Come on, Ed. Keep the door shut."

She moved along the bench towards Thorne, knowing the dreadful thing that was going to happen. Cameron had the door to the foodstore open. He was watching her enigmatically. She felt as though she were looking at a stranger. She shut her eyes tight as she heard the footsteps into the porch. She was shaking with fear yet the need to see and know was stronger. Cameron opened the back door. The two men shuffled into the kitchen, their burden hanging between them. She recognized nothing of the man she had known, neither the scorched skull that rolled so sickeningly nor the death mask beneath. Then mercifully the door was shut on it. Cameron's face was pitiless.

"Let's make the tour, Henry."

Thorne walked like a man on dry land after a long sea voyage. She heard them climbing the stairs. Chalice gaped.

"OK, Ed. No use you hanging round any more. Get weaving. I'll make my own way back. Tomorrow, prolly, late."

His partner hooked the spectacles over his ears. As far as he was concerned she might have been part of the kitchen furniture.

"All right, mate, keep in touch and take care of yourself. They're a right pair of lunatics."

Chalice clapped the other on the shoulder. "I know

what I'm doing. If you don't hear from me, day after tomorrow, latest, get down here in a hurry."

The younger man's blond hair was hidden under the cap. "I wish you well," he said formally and was gone. In another minute they heard the noise of the Humber going down the driveway. She bit her lip, trying to hide her growing terror.

Chalice spoke with rough sympathy. "There ain't nothing you can do except try to forget it."

The two men were coming down the stairs. She struggled against a fresh outburst of tears. Cameron's eyes were like the rest of his face, tired but dogged. He showed them the key to the back door, looking at her for what seemed an eternity.

"Use the windows if you feel like making for the cane brake. Breakfast's at eight and Mrs. Thorne's cook. No lights upstairs."

They filed after him, up a white-painted staircase to the second story. He halted in front of an open door. There was enough light to see his smile as he bowed.

"The bridal suite. Have a good trip."

The door shut. She found Thorne in the darkness, holding him tight as the key was turned in the lock from the outside.

HENRY CADWALLADER THORNE
23rd December

HE WOKE LIKE A CAT, his head completely station-
ary, only his eyes moving. His watch lay on the
bedside table. He read the hands in the pale morning
light. Nine minutes past seven. He shifted cautiously, raising himself on an elbow. Jamie was lying
on her side, hair fanning out over the pillow, her face
half-hidden. She had sobbed most of the night. Now
she was sleeping heavily, the sheet clutched to her
mouth stained with eyeblack.

He eased himself cautiously from the bed. The
boards creaked under the faded carpet as he put his
feet to the ground. The long oval mirror reflected the
four-poster bed with its dark-red fringe, the massive
tallboy and old-fashioned wardrobe.

The furniture and bric-a-brac were the relics of
Charles Gore, C.B.E. late Indian Civil Service, and
had come with the house. Benares brasswork, plastic
Buddhas, a teak chest filled with shot-gold saris, trash
bought from countless Red Sea bumboats.

He buttoned his pajama jacket, shivering as he
went to the window. Outside the trees and fences
sagged under the weight of the blizzard that had

blown for most of the night. Snow blurred the outlines of the barn and stable buildings. The tracks made by the Humber had been completely obliterated. The entire garden was an expanse of dazzling white under a lowering sky.

He tried the door leading into the corridor. It was still locked. He listened at the crack, hearing Chalice's cheerful cockney, the Canadian's deeper voice. He went into the bathroom. He was still there shaving when the bedroom door was thrown open. Cameron was wearing a roll-neck sweater and whipcord slacks. His magpie head glistened with water. His eyes were red and puffed as though sleep had eluded him. He glanced across at the sleeping woman.

"Get her out of that. Breakfast's in half an hour."

The door was shut. Thorne stood looking down at her, puzzled by the show of hostility the two of them were staging for his benefit. Long after she had gone to sleep, he'd lain awake with the blizzard battering against the window, seeking the solution. He needed no private detectives, no tape recordings to prove her deception. She had betrayed him cleverly and with enthusiasm. Now, with everything they wanted within their grasp, they were putting on an act that would have deceived anyone less credulous than himself.

He dressed slowly in a clean flannel shirt, the leather-patched jacket, the old comfortable trousers. He was tying his shoes when the answer came with almost mathematical certainty. *It wasn't an act.* He'd been underestimating the Canadian all along. The hatred was there — the violence and revenge motive — all these were constant. His error lay in a false assessment of their application. A simple shuffle of cards revealed the real order of play. Cameron's lead had been the ingenuous acceptance of the status quo. He'd taken Jamie back for just as long as it had suited him. Now he was through with her and she knew it. Odds on he'd told her as much yesterday at Bywater Mews, when he'd gone into the kitchen.

Liar, whore and hypocrite. He'd called her that openly. His contempt stemmed from the fact that he knew it was true. He'd known she'd change sides again and that this time it would be too late. First card played — first trick taken. The second trick was worth sixty-one thousand pounds. Ironic to think of it now — like him, Cameron must have always meant to get up from the game with all the table stakes. The Thornes he'd leave to each other. The last uncertainty was how Cameron intended to play the rest of his hand.

He sat on the side of the bed and touched Jamie's cheek with his fingers.

"Darling. Darling, wake up!"

She did so suddenly, sitting bolt upright, looking at him without recognition.

"It's twenty to eight," he told her. "Bruce was here. You're supposed to cook the breakfast."

She shut her eyes tight. Tears forced their way through the closed lids. He covered her mouth with his own. Last night the maneuver had worked as a substitute for explanations. It failed now. She pushed him away, pulling the hair out of her eyes.

"You didn't trust me — *why?* I'd have done anything for you, Henry. Anything."

He looked away, registering shame and despair. Cameron might be finished with her, he wasn't.

"I don't know how to say this, Jamie. That news bulletin you heard in the car last night — the robbery at the factory — that was us. Bruce, Robin — me. Don't ask for reasons or excuses — there isn't any time. All you've got to understand is this — unless you help me I'm going to prison. Or worse."

She shook her head violently. "I was wrong about Robin, wasn't I? It wasn't his idea at all — it was Bruce's. *God* what a fool I've been!"

He moved his shoulders hopelessly. "If it hadn't been for you I wouldn't have done it, I suppose. I've been living a lie for months — those trips abroad — this house. I trusted him instead of you and now it's too late."

She pulled his face round, forcing him to look at her. "It *isn't* too late. We'll go to the police together, darling. I'll tell them the truth — everything. They'll believe me — I *know* they will."

"I love you," he said. "And God knows I'm ashamed of what I've done to you. I'll go to the police but it isn't as easy as that. Your father was right, Jamie. Bruce is a paranoiac — a killer — and he's armed. We've got to get the gun away from him somehow."

She was out of bed and into her slacks in one movement. He heard her splashing in the bathroom. She
came out pinning her mass of hair into a scarf. She
wore no makeup. She came over to the bed where he
was sitting.

"What about the other man?"

He made a sign of negation. "He's a thug. He's
only here to help get rid of Robin's body. He'll do
anything Bruce says."

She looked at him with compassion. "As long as
you need me I'll help you — you know that."

He clutched her round the middle, his face against
the warmth of her belly.

"He's vicious and cunning, but he can make mistakes. We've got to show him everything his warped
mind wants to see. Fear — resignation. *That's* when
he'll make his mistakes. Do whatever he says, Jamie,
and take care."

As soon as he heard her going down the stairs he
opened the top drawer of the tallboy. The wallet
Kosky had sent him was hidden under the lining. He
riffed through the contents. Everything was there.
Airplane ticket and passport, an authorized copy of
a birth certificate — a sheaf of back-dated letters that
supported yet another identity. Henry Turberville,
bachelor and ornithologist. He looked round for
somewhere to secrete the wallet. It was certain that
Cameron would search the house as soon as he remembered. Luck had had it that last night he'd
wanted no lights upstairs. Thorne compressed his lips.
Without the gun Bruce shrank to life-size. He lifted

the mattress tentatively, then dropped it again. Cameron had learned too much to be bluffed by such an obvious hiding place. He discarded one alternative after another. The top of the wardrobe — the cistern — underneath the carpet. The thought came as he looked at the window. He raised the bottom sash. The kitchen was directly below. Cameron's voice drifted up, baiting and ironical. A four-inch ledge of snow covered the sill. He pushed the wallet well under it and tidied the edges. It was completely hidden. He lowered the window, satisfied. Bruce could tear the place apart now if he wanted. He walked down the stairs composing his features to the end-of-the-road look expected of him.

Daylight had given the kitchen new proportions, making it larger, brighter. Someone had turned on the central heating. The room was warm and pleasant, beyond the grip of winter. The refectory table was set for breakfast, coffee brewing on the stove. Jamie had a skillet of bacon in her hand. A cigarette dangled from her lips. She glanced at him warningly. Chalice and Cameron were sitting at the table side by side. Wet tracks led across the stone flags. One of them — or both — had been outside. Chalice looked up, spitting out a piece of apple core, his face moody.

Suddenly Cameron slammed his hand down on the table. "Do I *still* have to eat breakfast with that stink in my nostrils? Can't you go five minutes without a cigarette?"

Jamie's cheeks flushed. She dropped the cigarette

end on the floor and put her foot on it. Chalice yawned, looking up blankly at the ceiling.

"That's what I like, a nice friendly atmosphere. Morning, Professor, I trust I see you well?"

"Good morning."

"Have you got anything to dig with?"

Thorne sat opposite Cameron. The pale blue stare that greeted him was unfathomable.

"There are some gardening tools outside," he said. "In a shed in the stableyard."

He watched his wife carry the platter of bacon and eggs to the table. She set a tray with a cup, saucer and plate and started towards the door leading to the hall. Cameron's chin lifted.

"Where the hell do you think *you're* going?"

She stopped, looking him full in the face. "In one of the other rooms — I thought you might prefer it."

Chalice rose like a large tomcat being chivvied out of a favorite corner. He took the tray out of Jamie's hands and piled it with the rest of the breakfast things.

"You're getting on my wick — the lot of you. She doesn't want to eat here, we'll eat somewhere else. But I'm hungry."

He carried the tray into the sitting room. Thorne walked over to the roll-top desk and put his plate on the Swissair timetable. December gales had blown down the chimney since his last visit a month before. The velvet-covered sofa, the carpet and chairs were gray with wood ash. They ate like convicts living under a rule of silence, eyeing one another furtively. When they were done, Jamie collected the tray. The kitchen door shut behind her. It was two minutes to nine. Cameron switched on the radio, pacing about as he waited for the news. The weather forecast was gloomy. A blizzard had blanketed the West Country, disrupting rail and road traffic. More snow threatened with sub-zero temperatures from John o'Groats to the south coast. There was no further mention of the Palaton robbery. Cameron turned the set off. He was like a caged animal — ten paces, turn, another ten in the opposite direction, his eyes always on the ground. He stopped in front of the window.

"What lies beyond that hill?"

Thorne filled his pipe from a jar on top of the desk. He used the Swissair timetable as a spill to light it with.

"The village. About a mile away by the lane we took last night. The other way — through the woods are some people called Warren."

Chalice picked the dried egg off his stubbled chin. "Let's have a look at the churchyard. Remember what I told you?"

"What about the vicarage?" asked Cameron. "Is there anyone living there?"

Thorne tamped the tobacco into the bowl of his pipe. "The vicar and there's nothing he likes quite as much as minding other people's business."

"Uhuh," said Cameron. "Then you'll have to think again."

Chalice brooded. Thorne released a cloud of smoke, gambling deliberately.

"There's a place about ten miles away — Stowell Lake. It's on Forestry Commission land. I've fished there. The water's deep — I'd say thirty feet in some places — a silt bottom and no current."

Chalice sat up in his chair, exploring the white streak down the middle of his head.

"That's more like it."

Cameron's eyes were wide. "Cement. There's bound to be some building going on in the neighborhood — stores."

Chalice stretched ponderously, like a large brown bear. "I got news for you, mate. This kind of weather builders don't work. There's something keeps bothering me. I ain't heard even the faintest tinkle of money yet."

"The banks aren't open," said Cameron. "Maybe you'd rather forget it — there's still time."

Chalice fended off the suggestion with both hands. "Forget twenty thousand nicker — you must be joking! I was only asking. That's that, then. I'll go upstairs and see if me hens have laid."

As soon as he'd gone, Cameron shut the door. He jerked a finger at the phone on the bookcase.

"Call up and see if it's arrived."

The instrument was a dial-and-ask set. Thorne made a show of reluctance.

"This line's straight through to the local exchange. I thought you didn't want people to know the house was occupied."

Cameron's smile was satisfied. "They'll know George Watson's here, that doesn't bother me."

It was difficult not to laugh in his face. *They'll know George Watson's here!* He dialed O. A West Country voice came on the line almost immediately.

"Templecombe Station, Goods."

Thorne cleared his throat. "It's about a packing case that left Waterloo Station some time last night. It's addressed to George Watson and marked 'To be called for.' Can you tell me whether it's arrived?"

The voice was regretful. "The man in charge is having his brekfuss — I'm only the porter. But I wouldn't think so, sir. There's been nothing down from London since last night and the main line's blocked this side of Yeovil. They're working on it now."

Thorne put the phone down. He shrugged. "It's not there."

"I heard," said Cameron. "We've got time — we can wait. There's only one thing — remember that the train bit was your idea. If it falls apart on us, *you* pay the bills."

Thorne knocked his pipe out in the grate. "What am *I* supposed to do — control the weather as well?"

He realized, even as he spoke, that the words were as wrong as the tone he'd used. Cameron took him by the throat with both hands.

"*Do?*" he repeated savagely. "What the hell *can* you do! Go screw your wife."

His shove sent Thorne halfway across the room. He sprawled over the sofa and lay there protecting his head with both arms. He lifted himself cautiously, hearing Cameron running up the stairs. The Canadian was down again in a few minutes, with Chalice. Thorne stood behind the curtains watching the two men skirt the rhododendrons, heading for the stable-yard. Chalice was in his fur-lined coat, his trousers tucked into his socks. Cameron had taken the pair of waders from the hall cupboard. They crossed the tiny bridge over the stream and vanished from sight.

He turned away from the window telling himself that his brain still worked faster than Cameron's. He'd lost the inhibitions of a lifetime in the last twenty-four hours. It had been a simple enough lesson to learn. In a situation like this the use of violence was inevitable. The only thing to be feared was the detection of its use. Robin was already dead. Killing the others was the final insurance. Cameron was making it easy — literally digging his own grave.

His insistence on making the call to the station, for instance. The suggestion that had triggered the new plan. The girl at the exchange had certainly recognized the voice she knew as George Watson's. The few people who knew him in the neighborhood would remember him as the man who brought tragedy to the district. He imagined the cool impersonal voices in county drawing rooms.

A man who bought the Gore house a couple of years or so ago. We never actually met him, but Gillian heard that he used to have some very odd parties — people down from London, that sort of thing! Anyway, the house went up in flames one night.

Everyone in it was burned to death — four of them — this man Watson, a woman and two other men. Burned to a cinder — ghastly! Drunk? But of course — they found enough bottles to sink a battleship.

It had to be staged credibly. No marks of violence on the bodies — no bullet holes or cracked skulls. And it must be properly timed, early in the morning. The paneled house would go like a forest fire. Hidden as it was behind the hill, there was no one *to* see — and the nearest fire brigade was twelve miles away. The weakest link in the newly forged chain was the man who had gone back to London — Chalice's partner. But a slum thief like that would go to the police about as readily as he'd go to the public hangman. He'd probably get a gang together and start backtracking on Henry Thorne. By then it would be far too late — the metamorphosis would be complete. Thorne into Watson into Turberville.

A motor spluttered outside. He ran back to the window. There must have been enough charge in the battery to get the car going. The mini roared out of the stableyard with Cameron at the wheel. It ran down the slope almost as far as the gates then skated into the snowbank. Chalice ploughed in after it, climbing onto the front bumper and bouncing up and down. The front-wheel driven wheels showered him with snow. But the small car sank deeper in the drift.

Thorne spun round as the phone shrilled. He backed away from the window, keeping his eyes on the scene outside. He picked up the receiver. He heard a click but no one spoke.

"Squab Farm," he said in a low guarded voice.

Kosky's German was deliberate. "I tried to reach you last night. Mr. Smith telephoned. Do you know who I mean?"

The name drilled into Thorne's mind — pseudonym for Kosky's contact at the Yard — a clerk in the Criminal Records Office who notified Kosky whenever a major call for action was sounded at police headquarters. He was suddenly filled with foreboding.

"I know who you mean."

"Then pay attention. An anonymous letter was sent to our friends, giving the names and addresses of three men. Yours was one of them. Our friends found a typewriter. The type matches that on the letter. And they found a map. They would like to interview all three men."

Thorne broke out of a shocked silence. "Do they have complete authority?" It was better than "warrant of arrest" if anyone were listening.

Kosky was abrupt. "I do not know. But you will have to make other arrangements. I am no longer interested. I do not like anonymous letters."

The line went dead. Thorne put the phone down, his heart banging in its rib cage. Kosky's withdrawal was all the more significant because the Pole liked his percentages. He only went to ground when hounds were actually in sight. But there'd be another way of handling the money. The rest of his plan must wait in any case till the cash was in his possession.

There was movement through the window. He

peered out cautiously. The two men were plodding towards the stable. The mini was half-hidden in the snowbank. He hurried into the kitchen. Jamie was at the sink peeling potatoes. He put his fingers to his lips hearing the footsteps in the porch. Cameron came in alone, blood trickling from his right hand. He crossed to the sink and held his hand under the faucet. Jamie salted the potatoes and put the pan ready to boil on the stove. *The gas stove!* Thorne's fingers covered his mouth, as if the thought might show on his face. That was it, the gas stove. He'd seal the kitchen doors and windows and keep the three of them there at pistol-point. Afterwards he'd carry them upstairs, one by one.

"If you want anything for that hand, there's some stuff upstairs in my bathroom," he said.

Cameron flicked the blood away and licked the wound. He neither looked at Jamie nor used her name, aiming the word like a missile.

"Coffee!"

He went outside again, walking towards the barn, his clothing drab against the brilliant background. Jamie was still holding the potato knife, her mouth pinched with anger. He disengaged the knife from her fingers.

"Jamie," he pleaded. "You're not going to give up, are you?"

She shook her head slowly, watching the men outside. They carried shovels down the driveway and started digging out the wheels of the stalled car. She turned suddenly, twisting the wedding ring on her finger, staring at the closed door as though seeing the body that lay behind it.

"No. I'm not going to give up," she said in a low voice.

He suddenly wanted to take her by the throat as Cameron had taken him. He held her wrists instead.

"I bluffed with a bankrupt business — made a thief out of myself — because I love you, Jamie. Nothing else matters as long as you're on my side."

She looked at him, unsmiling and with troubled eyes. "It's true, isn't it?"

He took her gently by the arms. "I've thrown away everything — honor, loyalty — I've even forfeited your trust. Help me get these things back."

She shut her eyes tight. When she opened them again they were filled with pity.

"I will — of *course* I will. I'll phone the police now — while they're outside."

He stepped back, shaking his head. "Then they'll never see me alive — you can be certain of that. He'd shoot me out of hand, long before the police could do anything. He's insane, Jamie. Somehow we've got to get that gun away from him."

"Don't you think I've thought about it?" she said. "But *how*? He hates me even more than he hates you."

He touched her throat with the tips of his fingers, feeling the beating pulse under the fine skin. A little more pressure would find the arteries then his thumbs could dig in and paralyze them. It would all be too easy. She'd die like the whore she was, lips parted and flaunting her breasts. He took his fingers away.

"You're a woman."

She stared at him oddly. "That's right, I'm a woman. Tell me the truth — I can't stand any more lies — you think I've been having an affair with Bruce since our marriage, don't you?"

She was like a skilled exponent of judo, using her opponent's strength as a lever to vanquish him.

"I did," he answered. "But not any more."

Her smile was sad. "I knew it. The way you looked at me sometimes. Funny. You didn't trust me and in a way you're right. Not that I haven't been loyal to you. But — *your* love's uncomplicated — something that has integrity. The truth is that I've never known what I was looking for — a mirror, perhaps, that would tell me that I'm a nicer person than I really am. A shoulder to hold and to cry on. I don't know. But I *am* on your side, darling."

He lit a cigarette for her and drew small circles on the table with the burned end of the match. Expediency had recruited a dangerous ally in her. A ruthless and skilled actress. If it came off, Cameron's seduction would be her final triumph. He raised his head.

"Put some makeup on. The rest'll happen naturally. Answer when he talks to you. *Remind* him that you're a woman, defenseless but desirable."

She seemed to have difficulty with her choice of words, groping till she found the right ones.

"Henry — I don't feel ashamed — it somehow

evens things out. Do you know what I'm trying to say?"

The farce must go on, he thought. *That's what you're trying to say.*

He nodded. "You're going to save our lives, Jamie. It's as simple as that. That's what you're trying to say."

She opened the brown suede bag, making a mouth as she saw herself in the small hand mirror. She dabbed her neck and wrists with scent. He ducked down suddenly, sliding along the bench away from her.

"Get the coffee ready — they're going back to the stables."

Back in the sitting room, he knelt in front of the grate and started clearing out the ashes. There was coal and wood in the brass bucket. His gamble had paid off. They hadn't been able to move the mini, that much was certain. He'd have to keep them lulled with the promise of transport — a car capable of taking Robin's body through the snow as far as the lake. As he lit the fire, the phone rang yet again. He swung round, willing it to be a wrong number — an engineer's test call. The summons was persistent and peremptory. He took the receiver off the stand.

The speaker's voice held a touch of authority. "Is that Bruton seven-oh-seven, name of Watson?"

The wood crackled in the fireplace. "Seven-oh-seven," he said.

"This is Templecombe Goods Station. It's about a packing case from Waterloo — are you the gentleman who was inquiring this morning?"

175

"That's right."

"Well it's here all right, sir. Come on the last train through last night. My mate must have missed it."

Chalice and Cameron were crossing the grass between the stream and house. He hurried the words.

"I'm not sure when I'll be able to collect it. The roads round here are impassable."

The man sounded cooperative. "No trouble at all, sir. We've got plenty room here. The only thing to remember is that we're closed Christmas Day and Boxing Day."

"I'll be over as soon as I can," Thorne promised, a strange ringing in his ears. "And thanks for calling."

He saw himself in the mirror, smiling and triumphant. Home and dried. Or he would be as soon as he got the gun.

He rose obediently as Cameron shouted for him. The two men were in the kitchen, their faces bleak with cold and looking dispirited. Jamie added cream to the jug of coffee and set three mugs on the table.

"Shall I go upstairs and make the beds now?"

It was brilliant, he thought. The long-legged captive maiden, submissive and desirable. Cameron showed no sign of appreciating the performance.

"Sure," he said casually. "We'll have lunch at one. Corned beef hash with none of your artistic trimmings."

He poured a mug of coffee for Chalice and pushed another in Thorne's direction.

"The car's stuck in a drift. It'll stay there unless we can get a tractor."

Thorne cradled the mug in his hands, studying Cameron. The police would have a general description of him by now — from his landlord — someone else who lived in the house. But without a photograph they'd never be able to trace him further than Oakley Street.

"You're not making sense, Bruce," he said suddenly. "Don't you realize what you're doing? Half-strangling me one minute and expecting cooperation the next!"

"We'll let that statement go," Cameron said.

The rift between them was so wide that Chalice's presence was forgotten. There was a touch of the old Thorne in his orderly marshalling of the facts.

"We can't *afford* to let it go. You've taken control but my interests are the same as yours — for the moment at least. They have to be, Bruce. Don't you see that? Whether they stay the same is something that depends entirely on you."

Chalice was scraping his spoon round the bottom of his mug, licking it thoughtfully. Cameron shook his head.

"It's no good, Henry. The old magic's gone."

He repeated the words without rancor. "The old magic? Only a few hours ago we were risking our liberty together. What's happened since then to turn you against me? I mean what's *really* happened — not just what you imagine? I'm on your side. I have to be."

177

Cameron slid his coffee mug along the table. "There's nothing in this world that puts us on the same side and you know it."

Chalice pulled the wrapper from one of his panatellas. He made a wad of the cellophane and fired it at the sink.

"Shalala*la!*" he said. "I'm beginning to wonder what I'm doing here."

Cameron's face stiffened. "You *know* what you're doing here. It isn't affected by anything he says."

"I wouldn't be too sure about that," Thorne said. His quiet manner had the result he hoped for. Both men were watching him closely. He lit his pipe, dragging out the ritual.

"What would you say if I told you I could get hold of a Landrover?"

A thermostat control cut in, sending oil blasting through the furnace. Cameron's eyes were suspicious.

"Where?"

He lied fluently. "The other side of the hill. My nearest neighbors people called Warren. They keep it to pull their horsebox. I talked to the man's wife while you were trying to get the mini going."

Chalice's shrug was expressive. "Then we're in business. Those things'll go through four feet of mud."

Cameron looked considerably less satisfied. "Who else did you phone, Henry?" he asked softly.

Thorne gestured at Chalice, lifting his hands in despair. "You see what I mean? *Nobody*, Bruce. I know the Warrens. I've fished with the Colonel.

And I've borrowed his Landrover before. There's no problem there."

The pale stare probed Thorne's face. "Shall I tell you what comes next, Henry? You want to go and fetch it, don't you?"

Thorne shifted his shoulders. "Warren's in Bristol, as it happens. And his wife doesn't know where the Landrover keys are. He's due back tomorrow. I thought *you'd* have ideas how we could collect it."

Cameron pounced, as quickly as Thorne had expected. "How's the Colonel going to get himself from the station, ride one of his horses?"

Thorne allowed himself a thin smile of triumph. "The suggestion was that I fetched him. Mrs. Warren's going to telephone to Bristol tonight. He'll tell her where the keys are."

The house, name and horses were all genuine. If Cameron wanted to crawl through the snow playing Indians, let him.

Help came from an unexpected quarter, qualified but definite. Chalice's air was one of professional disillusionment.

"Up to now I ain't lost nothing but my time — and a few quid expenses. It won't make or break me. But that's all I *am* going to lose. The Professor says tomorrow. OK. Tomorrow it is. But if that body ain't shifted by then I'm off." He made it plain that as far as he was concerned anyone with sense would be with him.

Cameron refilled his mug. "Do you mean that?"

"I mean it," Chalice answered. He took a duster

from the dresser and flicked it over his shoes. He straightened up, waving the duster to give his words emphasis. "I'm getting a feeling about this caper that ain't a healthy one. This isn't a wake. Only a bleeding bunch of nuts sit round a dead man, *waiting*. I'll give it till tomorrow night. No Landrover, Harry-boy's off. Don't worry about me and Eddie. Send us a letter from the nick."

Thorne was watching the pair of them cautiously. Whoever Cameron used the gun on it wouldn't be Chalice — and Chalice knew it. The Canadian's grin was reluctant, but it broke the sudden tension.

"OK. It's a deal. Either way, it's a deal."

Chalice reached high, like a man preparing to dive. "That's that then. I'd better whip these whiskers off. Who's got a razor?"

"There's one in the bathroom." Cameron showed no sign of leaving Thorne alone.

They heard Chalice whistling his way upstairs. Thorne spoke in an undertone.

"I didn't want to say so in front of him but the case is at the station."

Cameron advanced towards him, treading softly. "How do you know?"

Thorne shrugged. "They phoned from the station. The man made a mistake."

Cameron tapped him on the shoulder. "See *you* don't make one. From here on in, keep away from the phone unless I say so. And don't put your nose outside the house."

Thorne waited till Cameron took his hand away.

The moves were predetermined now. He'd gained a day and a half in which to get the gun. He was fairly sure of Jamie; less sure of Bruce; certain of himself.

"You've managed to give Chalice the impression that he's on a sinking ship. Sometimes I think that what you really want is failure — the whole deal to end in disaster."

Cameron went over to the refrigerator. He punched a couple of holes in a can of beer, drank it and wiped his mouth on the back of his hand.

"Then you'd better do some rethinking. Never mind about Chalice. He stays or he goes, what the hell. But if the ship *does* go down you and I go down with it."

Thorne spread his hands. He was sure that his hunch was correct. *He* was the only one Cameron would use the gun on. As a last resort, possibly, but use it he would.

Cameron stepped on the pedal, dropping the empty beer can into the garbage pail.

"Don't forget what I said — keep in the house."

He went out by the door leading into the hall, the gun bulging in his back pocket. Thorne heard him moving about in the sitting room. Only one thing stopped the Canadian from putting him under restraint — the fact that Cameron wanted George Watson to be available to take any phone calls. He put the memory of Kosky's message out of his mind hurriedly. Cameron was going up the stairs. Thorne waited till he heard him in the corridor then tiptoed across the hall into the sitting room. The desk drawers had been ransacked — books pulled from the shelves. He sat in front of the brightly burning fire, listening to the pandemonium going on upstairs. He heard Cameron's biting voice, Jamie's subdued answer.

His pipe had gone out. He sucked on the cold sour stem. Cameron would be by the bed now. Only a thin pane of glass separating him from the hidden wallet. Thorne had a strange feeling that his life depended on the next few minutes.

JAMESON THORNE
23rd December

S HE SAT DOWN on the bed, her legs weak and trembling. He'd stormed in like a fury, face icy, telling her to stay where she was. Then he'd searched the room, sparing her no indignity, ripping the sheets from the bed, overturning the mattress, wrenching up the carpet with such force that the nails came with it. He'd stopped in the doorway when he'd done, his eyes relentless.

"I always told you — anything you start, I'll finish."

She picked up the clothes scattered over the floor and remade the bed. She might have had a chance even yesterday, but it was surely too late now. She prayed with a sense of shame because there was nothing else left to do. The prayer was without form or sound, a plea to something stronger than herself. But there was no miracle, only the noise of Bruce tearing apart the neighboring bedroom.

She stood in front of the long oval mirror. The pale gray light filtering into the bedroom was kind to her face. He'd called her a whore — perhaps that was the answer. Perhaps she could still save Henry and herself by being what Bruce wanted her to be. She unbuckled her hair, dragging the blond mass behind her ears. She had worn it like that the first day they'd met, strangers at a Chelsea party.

He had been standing alone, glowering across the smoky room, a tall man in a flannel suit. Their eyes had met and she'd watched him put his glass down. She knew instinctively that he would come over and speak to her. He pushed his way through the crowd and lifted her hand to his lips. He made the gesture easily, without affectation. His smile came belatedly, as though he'd suddenly recalled the necessity to look pleasant.

"I'm Bruce Cameron. If I'd seen you before, I'd remember."

His voice was slightly slurred with drink, the accent North American. His eyes were the palest blue and without expression. His short black hair was peppered with gray over the ears. He looked and smelled clean. His smile widened as she inspected him, as if he was reading her mind.

"I'm not respectable if that's what's bothering you — who the hell *is* in this place?"

She laughed in spite of herself and told him her name. The sound seemed to please him. He repeated it twice.

"Do you know you have the most beautiful ears I've ever seen, Jamie?"

She touched them self-consciously. "That's a pleasant thing to hear, especially as they're the only pair I have."

He took hold of her wrist, gently disengaging her fingers from the glass.

"Tell me something, Jamie. How are you on the nation's need of fantasy — or do you feel that it has no social significance?" He blocked a hiccough hurriedly.

"I'm an art student," she said.

He lurched slightly, clapping his hand to his forehead. "My God — don't tell me I've picked up an intellectual! *Look* at me, Jamie. You see the greatest suspense writer Canada ever produced — unfortunately I'm unpublished. What do you say — shall we cut this scene and eat someplace?"

She searched the room for the man who had brought her to the party. He was flat on his back, head resting in the lap of a girl wearing a green wig. Without a doubt he was still holding forth on the importance of the navel in art. She smiled at Cameron and picked up her bag.

"You do me a kindness, sir. Pray lead the way."

They ate at a Russian restaurant near the river. Rather *she* ate, he just drank, waving away each course as it was brought. His voice slowed as the tempo of the balalaikas quickened. Suddenly he lifted his head and she saw there were tears in his eyes.

"God help us, I think I love you, Jamie."

She had gone to bed that night, disturbed, elated — half-expecting never to see him again. He'd appeared the next day, staggering under an enormous sheaf of roses. Two weeks later she had moved into the basement flat at Oakley Street.

She let her hair fall forward and buckled it on the side, the way she'd been wearing it for the last year. He'd never understood the real reason for her running away — that it would have been impossible for either of them to forget what she'd done with Henry. Ironic that now, for the second time in her life, she was preparing to do something that could be a shameful memory.

Preparing? she asked herself hopelessly. Wasn't that wishful thinking? If Henry was right, everything that Bruce had said to her in the kitchen the day before had been part of his plan to destroy them — the viciousness of a man completely wrapped up in hatred. She still found the idea difficult to accept. She'd known him violent, vain, obstinate to the point of stupidity — but never deceitful. But he might have changed. She had a quick feeling of guilt. If he *had* changed it would be because of her. She'd lied to him about her feelings just as she'd lied to her husband. The truth had always been that she loved love. Now she wasn't even sure about that any more.

She made up her mouth and eyes, using the bold lines he liked. If it happened, it would be worse than rape — worse than going to bed with a complete stranger. She saw herself cast in a drama that she alone could avert from becoming tragedy.

She went to the door. The household seemed to have settled down into an uneasy avoidance of one another. Bruce was somewhere along the corridor, Chalice in the kitchen. Henry was probably in the sitting room. She turned away, wondering what she would do if the gun were in her hands. She knew vaguely that she'd have to convince Bruce that she'd use it.

More than that she didn't know. Her instinct demanded the intervention of someone stronger than herself, stronger than all of them. If God was deaf then perhaps the police. Tears were ruining her eye-black. She dabbed at them with her handkerchief, staring through the window. The sky hung low, dull against the frosted brilliance of the ground. A fresh flurry of snow after breakfast had filled in all the car tracks. She stayed perfectly still as a sparrow lit on the window ledge. The thick crust of snow outside supported its tiny body. Seeing her, the bird rose, wings whirring. Its trailing legs broke the crust of snow. Something caught her eye — something blue, pushed under the snow. She lifted the window quietly, thinking that this might be what Bruce had been looking for. If so, it was better that she had it. She carried the plastic wallet to the bed, sat down and opened it. The first thing she saw was a first-class ticket from London to Zurich, open dated. The name on it meant nothing to her — Henry Turberville. The same name showed in the window of a brandnew British passport. She flicked over a couple of pages. Her husband's picture stared back at her blandly. She let the passport fall in her lap, the pulse beating faster in her throat. She opened the last document. It was a letter written under the heading of a Belgravia estate agent. She read it, framing the words with her lips.

20th October, 1965

Dear Mr. Thorne:

We are obliged for your recent telephone call. With reference to your inquiry we would now inform you that your solicitors, Messrs. Barr and Belfrage, have completed the title deeds relative to the freehold of number twenty Bywater Mews, S.W.3. These documents are in our possession and will be passed on to our client, Mr. Walter Garry. We have therefore instructed the National Provincial Bank (South Kensington Branch) to transfer the sum of £18,500 (eighteen thousand, five hundred pounds) to Messrs. Barr and Belfrage for your account.

We note further that possession has been granted to our clients as from January first, nineteen hundred and sixty-six.

Yours faithfully,
for Clive Kelvin Associates

She picked up the passport again, looking at her husband's photograph, stunned. The face continued to wear its economical smile. She read the letter through twice, beyond tears and strangely calm — almost as if she were under sedatives. The deception was somehow easier to take because of its enormity. There was no room left for doubt. He'd tricked, betrayed and deceived her and that was that. The sale of the house over her head was somehow the last straw — worse even than his desertion — an act of implacable cruelty committed by a monster.

She got up unsteadily and went into the bathroom.

Leaning over the basin, she vomited violently. After a while she rinsed her mouth and washed her face and hands. She applied fresh makeup with careful skill — as if above all she needed to look her best in the next few minutes.

The house had fallen completely silent. She started down the stairs, steadying herself against the banister rail. Her husband was sitting in front of the fire, reading. He looked up, smiling, as she came into the room. She walked towards him, slowly, fighting a fresh bout of nausea. She took her hand from behind her back and threw the wallet by his feet.

"You're . . ." She stopped, betrayed by the tremor in her voice. She was unable to bring herself to use his name. She found new courage. "I can only say you're inhuman. Not fit to live."

He picked the travel wallet from the floor. The pallor left a stark bridge of freckles across his nose.

"Listen to me and don't be a bloody little fool! What did you expect me to do — tell you that I'd sold number twenty — what would you have said? Don't you see that I had to go on like that once I'd started — pretending that everything was all right — for your sake as much as for mine?"

She looked at him steadily. "The ticket to Zurich — the passport in another name — the whole scheme to abandon me — was that for my sake too?"

His features were molded in a defiant sort of dignity. "You seem to be forgetting something. I'm a thief. There was a good chance that I might have been arrested leaving the country. What did you want me to do — involve you in it too? I happen to love you. When the danger was over I was going to send for you."

The smile was sincere, the voice frank but there was nothing he could do about his eyes.

She took a long deep breath. "You must be the most loathsome man on earth. Killing's too good for you." She tore the wedding ring from her finger and flung it at him.

His movement was quick but hers was quicker. She twisted out of his clutch and ran out into the hall, screaming. The noise shattered the stillness of the house. The response was immediate. Chalice burst through the kitchen door. Cameron came down, flying the stairs in four enormous bounds. He skated across the hall, tugging at his pocket. He had the gun out before he reached the sitting room door. He went into the room as if testing rotting floorboards. She heard something crash, her husband's shout of pain. The first thing she saw was Thorne on his knees, swaying with fogged eyes. Chalice picked up the chair and set it on its legs. He glanced from his clenched fist to the lump growing on Thorne's chin, clicking his tongue reprovingly.

"Halfway out the winder, the Professor was."

Thorne dragged himself upright painfully. His blurred eyes found hers and stayed there. Cameron looked from one to the other, nose thinned, flaring the answer to his question.

"What the hell's going on round here?"

Her legs went suddenly. She groped for the sofa behind her and denounced her husband without pity.

"Make him show you what he's got in his pocket — *make* him!"

Cameron poked the barrel of the gun in Thorne's direction. "Let's have it."

She was watching Thorne closely, sensing the cunning that ran in his brain.

"Go on," she challenged. "Tell him what you told me."

Thorne fingered his bruised chin furtively. Somehow he managed to look almost convincing.

"Watch her, Bruce," he said. "She's just found out something that's shaken her rigid. I'm leaving her for the same reason that you did. She's a whore. A tramp who's slept all over London. Men living in the mews, friends of mine — Robin — even her hairdresser." He gave Cameron the wallet with a smile.

She sat bolt upright, gripping the edge of the sofa, knees very close together. It was terribly important to her that they knew the truth about this foulness.

"Do *you* believe that?" she asked Cameron.

Cameron shoved a hand through his hair, his eyes bitter.

"What's it matter what I believe? What the hell *is* it you want from me?"

She shook her head, her eyes burning. Pity — forgiveness — the chance to take the bitterness out of his face. But there was no answer.

"Nothing," she said in a small voice. "Nothing at all."

Chalice picked up the passport, holding it against the light. He examined Thorne's picture, minutely, running a finger over the embossed stamp clipping its edge. His judgment was unqualified.

"That's a bit of Kosky's gear — two hundred and fifty quid's worth."

He gave the passport to Cameron who took his time with it. The Canadian studied each document in turn, mouth set in deep-graven lines. He looked at Thorne, his eyes bright with hostility.

"What a creep you are. You didn't even leave her the house. What was she supposed to live on?"

Her husband hadn't given up the fight. "Charm," he said. "The way she's always done."

A coal collapsed in the grate sending sparks shooting up the soot-encrusted chimney. Chalice walked over to the window. He stood with his back to them, considering the expanse of snow. He turned round and balled his heavy shoulders.

"I've had enough, mate," he said to Cameron.

The Canadian put the gun away as if making a point. "Maybe you're right. Anyway you've got no contract with me any longer. Go whenever you like and take her with you."

Chalice looked vaguely embarrassed. "It's just that I've got a feeling — you know how it is. You don't want to come with me, Canada?"

Cameron moved his head from side to side with the blind obstinacy that had always maddened her.

"I'm staying."

Chalice's hands spread in a gesture of resignation. "You know what you're doing, mate. Is it all right for me to phone Eddie?"

Cameron's smile was fleeting. "You *bet* I know what I'm doing. Let *him* get the number."

He lit a cigarette and sat on the arm of a chair. Beyond reach of anything, she thought suddenly. Anything and anyone. Chalice shoved the phone hard against Thorne's chest.

"Behave yourself," he growled. "You ain't at the top of my popularity poll neither."

Thorne seemed to have shrunk. His nose was peaked, his eyes furtive. He repeated the number and hung up. The lines must have been restored. The call came through almost immediately. Chalice snatched the phone, speaking in a jargon that was incomprehensible to her. He put the handset back on the bookcase, his face unusually sober.

"Eddie saw Kosky an hour ago. You're on the trot, mate. Someone sent a letter to the law, shopping the three of you for the Palaton job. The Heavy Mob turned your gaffs over nine o'clock this morning. They found a map in some drum in Kensington. And they took your typewriter away."

Cameron's face had drained of color. "What about *him?*" He was staring at Thorne.

Chalice made a sign of dissent. "Nothing. His place was clean. Old Bill's looking for all three of you but you're top of the list. You and the other geezer."

Cameron pitched his cigarette end into the fire, his voice strangely calm.

"Why did you do it, Henry?"

Thorne fended off the accusation, his expression a grotesque parody of innocence.

"Me?" he protested. "Are you out of your mind, Bruce? It doesn't even begin to make sense."

Cameron's indictment was inexorable. "It does to me. You typed that letter on my machine. You knew exactly what the police would do with it. You planted the second set of keys and you planted the map on Robin. When he died you had to start thinking again."

She studied her husband with loathing. His face told her that he was guilty even of this ultimate infamy. Chalice moved with surprising speed, putting his burly body between the other two men. Cameron's smile belied the twitch in his cheek.

"Don't worry. I'm not going to touch the bastard."

Chalice looked at his watch, mopping the back of his neck with the silk handkerchief.

"They've cleared the main roads. Eddie's already on his way. He says he can make it in three hours. I told him we'd cut through the woods and wait by the signpost — the one where we turned off by the bridge. There's room for you, Canada."

Cameron lit a fresh cigarette. "You'd better get your things together, Jamie."

"No!" she said desperately. She stood, trying for words that would break the barrier between them.

"No, you come with us! It doesn't matter about love — we need each other. Something else'll grow if we work at it. We've got to *try* — don't you see that?"

His head drooped for a moment. He raised it, looking at her as if concerned with her lack of understanding.

"You left *me*, Jamie. I didn't leave you. I'm not going to kill him. I'm going to make him suffer in the way he really appreciates — I'm going to leave him penniless. Not for your sake, nor for Robin's, but for *mine*."

Thorne's eyes were on the ground between his feet. She went by without looking at him, crossing the room to Cameron, ready to hold or be held. His eyes gave her no encouragement.

"We can start all over again," she pleaded. "We can *do* it. Some country where they'll never find us — somewhere in the sun. We can get jobs — you can write. This man'll help us get away."

Chalice spoke with rough, exasperated kindness. "You know that, mate. Forget about the money. I'll ship the pair of you out under the Old Pal's Act."

Cameron was unmoved. "All I want from you is a straight answer. How long have I got — what sort of chance is there?"

Chalice thought for a moment. "You're not in trouble yet. They ain't got your picture and you've got no form. They don't really know who they're looking for, do they? You're safe enough here. It's when you start dodging about you're going to have to start worrying. And if they *do* get you, mate, remember what Harryboy told you. They'll give you all the chances in the world to shop yourself. They'll bring you tea when you're thirsty and a smoke when you need one. They'll tell you what a mug you are and that all they want is help you. Stand for that and you'll be eating porridge for the next ten years. Keep your mouth shut and I can send you a dozen mouth-pieces who'll have you out of there before your name dries on the charge sheet. That ain't your problem — *he* is."

Cameron turned a somber eye on Thorne. "Fair enough. Is there any way of reaching you in a hurry? Somewhere safe."

Chalice scribbled a number on a piece of paper and gave it to the Canadian.

"Don't go near that club," he warned. "And don't go near Kosky. Keep off the streets in the daytime. Use taxis. If you've got to hang about, go in the British Museum. It's the safest place in London."

"I'll come alone if I do come," said Cameron.

"Let's hope so," said Chalice fervently. "And get rid of that bit of paper. Telephone as soon as you're ready. I'll get the message inside the hour. Bring one suitcase. If you have the wind behind you, you'll be in Capetown next time you see the light of day, with an entry stamp on your passport. That suit you?"

Cameron's eyes were steady. "That suits me."

She made one final attempt, knowing that if this failed she would never see him again.

"*Please*, Bruce."

"Only on my terms, Jamie. And they're tough. It's too late for anything else. You stay here with me. And you take the same chances that I do — share the risks as well as the benefits."

Something in his face told her that he was testing her — that he knew she would never agree — that he didn't even want her to. She had said goodbye to so much that was happy, a year ago. To do it again was heartbreaking.

"I can't, Bruce," she said quietly. "You know I can't. I'll go with you but not with money that you've stolen."

He lifted a hand and let it fall. "The way the ball bounces. Let your bank know where you are. OK?"

It was a long time since she'd seen him smile like this — without bitterness or irony.

"I will," she promised. They would go on in this way, exchanging furtive messages until he was finally smuggled out of the country. She knew that what was happening was inevitable. She could never have gone through life, a fugitive from justice, afraid of every knock at the door, every ring of the telephone. But there was something else that she knew — for the rest of her life she'd have him on her conscience.

He crossed the room to her husband and his smile was gone. "It's the end of the line, Henry. Time to pay for your ride."

She could see the sweat in the roots of her husband's hair as he inclined his head like a man about to be decapitated.

"Where does he bank?" Cameron asked her. His face gave no clue to his question.

"Barclay's, Piccadilly," she answered.

"And you?"

Her voice was barely audible. "You know where I bank."

Cameron's hand caught Thorne under the chin, jerking up his head.

"Where's the money you got for the house? Don't bother lying. You're going to be here with me when I find out the truth."

Thorne's neck was stretched as far as it would go. It was difficult for him to answer.

"The bank," he managed to say.

Cameron propelled him to the desk and shoved him down in the chair.

"It better had be. Start writing. Dear Mr. — whatever the manager's name is. Head it Twenty Bywater Mews."

Thorne made no move, sitting with his hands in his lap. His head rocked as Cameron cuffed him a couple of times. The Canadian pushed pen and paper in front of Thorne. His voice was ice cold.

"I said I wouldn't kill you. But step out of line and you'll wish that I had. I'll take your nails out one by one with a pair of pliers."

She tried to lift herself on unsteady legs, her stomach rebelling. Chalice pushed her down again. "Let them alone."

Her husband's face was livid save for the marks left by Cameron's palms. He picked up the pen, wrote something on the paper and waited. Cameron looked over Thorne's shoulder, dictating:

Dear Mr. Balding:

I shall be leaving England and wish therefore to close my account with you. Please transfer all funds to my wife's account at the following bank and address:

> Mrs. H. C. Thorne
> c/o Lloyd's Bank Ltd.
> Sloane Square
> S.W.3

By "all funds" I mean any credit balance you hold for me whether in the form of collateral or credits on deposit or in my current account.

This transfer must be effective immediately and you will accept this letter as your sole and final authority to act in this matter.

> Signed,
> Henry Cadwallader Thorne

He brought the letter over to her. "Is that his normal signature?"

She nodded. Cameron read the letter through again, sealed it in an envelope and smiled like a man about to tell a good joke.

"You just paid one fare stage. There are a couple more coming up." He gave the envelope to Chalice. "See that gets to the bank first thing tomorrow morning. It's one letter I wouldn't want lost."

Chalice dropped the envelope in an inside pocket. "It'll be there, mate."

Cameron stood for a while, a tall lonely man looking at her enigmatically.

"You'd better go now," he said quietly. "Fix something to eat. We've got things to talk about."

BRUCE CAMERON

23rd December

I T WAS ALREADY DARK in the sitting room with fire-light striking ruddy reflections from the wall paneling. The sullen sky outside seemed to have dropped much lower in the past hour. A cold draft was blowing through the open window but he felt insulated against all physical weaknesses, beyond pain and hunger. He'd barely touched the food Jamie had prepared. Now the Scotch and water was getting its work in.

He was alone with everyone in the house accounted for. Thorne was locked in the hall cloakroom and wouldn't be going anywhere in a hurry. The door was three inches thick and there were iron bars set in the window. The last time he'd seen him, Chalice had been stretched out on the bed reading *Tom Brown's Schooldays*. Jamie had stayed in her room since lunchtime. It was just as well. It was no good thinking about her any more. She belonged to the past. So many things seemed to belong to the past — nothing to the present or future.

The loneliness of the house, the shifting snow on the roof — above all the feeling that there was no place where he was welcome — pulled back the memory of the wooden manse in the grip of a Saskatchewan winter. He'd sat with his packed bag between his legs, facing his father across the spartan study, hearing the last bitter denunciation.

You're a wastrel, Bruce, a disgrace to your name. You've broken your mother's heart, but you'll not break mine. Get out and never come back and God have mercy on your miserable hide.

He remembered the gaunt Highland head with its burning eyes, the pinched white lips, the shaking outstretched hand pointing at the door. The whole scene had been lifted straight out of a Victorian melodrama. And what it all added up to really was a couple of drunken brawls, a night in the lock-up — a paternity suit brought by a girl who'd lost her virginity to a bicycle seat called Joe, three years before. Big-league stuff supposed to send him straight to hell.

He lit a cigarette. For most of his life he'd done what he wanted and most of the time he'd believed he was right. He could do without mercy, God's *and* Jamie's. Direction was what he needed. His real headache was what to do with Thorne. He accepted Chalice's professional assessment of his chances. But time was running out on him and he couldn't stay holed up indefinitely.

He pulled the gun out of his pocket, checking the ammunition clip for the twentieth time. The idea came suddenly — giving him a strange sense of relief. You could only destroy a man once but at least you could do it completely. And that was what he really wanted to do. His victory over Thorne was still a hollow one. But what if he surrendered himself to the police — told them the whole story and returned the money. He'd go to jail for sure, but Thorne would go with him. The Staunch Heart and Faithful Comrade, stripped of everything — money, wife and liberty.

He rammed the clip back, hearing someone coming down the stairs, and slipped the gun back in his pocket. His last thought on the subject was that there was still time to make up his mind. Chalice opened the door. He was wearing Thorne's waders. He looked down at Cameron and shrugged.

"That's it then, mate. We'd better get going. It'll take us the best part of an hour to walk through them woods. You haven't changed your mind about coming?"

It was hard to take offense yet Chalice's persistence was beginning to irritate him. "I haen't changed my mind," he said.

Chalice dropped the pair of shoes in Cameron's lap. "Then that's all I can do for you, chum."

The uppers were scuffed and ringed with water stains, the plugs still in the soles. He shook his head wearily.

"Take them away. I don't need that crap."

Chalice moved swiftly, pinning Cameron back in the chair with one hand, wrenching off the Canadian's shoes with the other. He threw them on the fire, standing over Cameron while they burned. A stink like a glue-factory filled the room. Chalice stepped back, breathing heavily.

"Don't make me tie them on your feet."

Cameron lifted a hand in token of submission. He pulled on the shoes and knotted the laces. He'd written about people like this, not knowing that they really existed. Men living beyond the laws of society yet bound by a code of their own that for them was equally inflexible. It was hard to know what to say.

Chalice's dark face still brooded. "Why don't you give me that pistol? You don't need it. I'll dump it for you."

This time he was making no concessions. "No dice, you made your point."

Chalice's smile flashed his gold fillings. "I'm going to wind up reading about you in the Sunday newspaper, that's a laydown."

They both turned as Jamie opened the door. Her hair was tied in a scarf, her coat buttoned as high as it would go. Chalice took the suitcase from her. He gave Cameron his hand.

"So long then, mate. And be lucky."

They heard him go through into the kitchen and open the back door. An icy draft reminded them that he was waiting. Cameron worried his lip with his teeth, looking at her red swollen eyes. She made no pretense to hide the fact that she'd been crying.

"Goodbye, Jamie," he said carefully.

She raised herself on her toes, touching his cheek with her lips. Her voice was as formal as his own, the voice of a small girl remembering her party manners.

"Goodbye, Bruce. And thank you."

She broke away swiftly and ran from the room. He dropped into the chair again, forcing himself to stay away from the window. The mirror over the fireplace reflected the bushes outside. They came into view, Chalice pulling back the snow-laden branches so that she could pass. As they passed the sitting room window, Cameron lifted his hand but neither of them looked back. A few minutes and they were lost in the wooded slopes beyond the barn.

There was an uncanny stillness in the house as if the chill creeping through the back door had completely immobilized all trace of life. He got up slowly, brushing the ash from his trousers. He walked over to the desk, moving stiffly in the unfamiliar shoes. There was a clear imprint on the blotter of the letter Thorne had written to the bank. He tore the sheet out and ripped it in small pieces. *Goodbye, Bruce and thank you.* He wanted her gratitude no more than her mercy.

He tipped the bottle of Scotch, poured himself two fingers and drank it neat. The liquor made a pool of warmth in his stomach. He hesitated with the cork in his fingers. He rammed it back firmly into the neck of the bottle. Not now, later, maybe. His brain had to stay sharp. And sooner or later he must eat. He went out to the hall. Something white lay on the stair carpet. He picked up the handkerchief, recognizing the scent. He crumpled the square of linen into a ball and tossed it away. This sort of thing would go on — with every sense tricking him into remembering her. A place, a song, a head of swinging blond hair.

Somehow he had to find a way of beating it. If love or hate wasn't the answer, what the hell *was*. The book said "time" — "indifference" — as if you grew them like new toenails.

He closed the back door and came back into the hall. He swung round looking at the locked cloakroom. The sound was unmistakable, the gurgle of a man strangling. He spun the key and threw the door wide. Thorne was hanging with his face to the window. One end of his belt was round his neck, the other fastened to one of the iron bars. His feet dangled inches from the floor. The back of his neck was a dull scarlet. There was no time to think, no knife to cut the belt. He grabbed at Thorne's legs, waiting to take the weight from his neck. As he bent down he saw what had been hidden from him. Thorne's right hand was flat against his breast, holding the belt under his chin, supporting his body.

Cameron swerved but too late. Thorne spun on the strip of leather, lashing out with both feet. His heels found their mark high between Cameron's legs, thudding home with sickening impact. Cameron fell sideways, his nails scraping down the wall. He writhed on the floor, crouched in fetal position. Part of his pain-wracked brain sensed Thorne land beside him, erect and free of the belt. The second kick took Cameron high on the temple. The shock was merciful, putting an end to his agony.

It seemed a long time later when he opened his eyes. A foul taste filled his mouth. He was lying on the sitting room floor, face pressed into his vomit. He rolled away, groaning. It was dark outside. The only light in the room came from the flames leaping in the chimney.

"What was the expression, Bruce — 'the end of the ride'?"

The voice had the thin rectitude of a judge about to pronounce the death sentence. He strained his eyes, trying to trace the source. They found Thorne sitting deep in the armchair, legs crossed, sighting down the barrel of the gun.

"You're very silent suddenly, aren't you?" he taunted.

Cameron wiped his mouth on his sleeve, his brain driving his muscles to respond. He could live forever with the pain between his legs if the Fate Sisters would grant him one chance.

Thorne raised the gun an inch, training the muzzle at Cameron's head.

"What happened to the man of action — my wife's benefactor? It's just as well she's not here, isn't it. She wouldn't be feeling so happy about her chances. You realize that I'll cancel that letter first thing in the morning, of course."

He dragged himself up on his knees, bringing himself a little nearer the poker in the grate.

"You'll never get away with it," he croaked.

Thorne tilted his head back and laughed. "Vintage Warner Brothers — Bogart, Greenstreet and Nolan. What won't I get away with?"

Cameron hurled himself sideways, grabbing at the

poker. He scrambled up, chopping it down at Thorne's wrist. The gun jumped in the Englishman's hand before the blow landed. A shell smacked into the wall paneling. A book fell to the floor. Cameron's ears rang. His nose filled with the stink of burned cordite. He sneezed violently. Thorne whipped behind the armchair.

"Another inch and you've had it," he said shakily. "Drop the poker and get down on your stomach — hands behind your back."

He stretched himself out on the carpet. Cord bit into his wrists, looped around his throat. The automatic was jammed against his right ear.

"On your knees."

He struggled up. He felt the cord knotted behind his ankles, his wrists dragged down to meet them. A shove toppled him sideways, trussed like a chicken. Thorne hooked a hand in the rope and dragged Cameron across the hall into the cloakroom.

"This is a good place to think, too," he said sarcastically. "Try writing the end of the story."

The door closed, taking the light with it. He lay quite still, tracking Thorne into the kitchen. A minute or so later, something bumped on the stairs. After a long while, he heard the soft squeak of Thorne's rubber soles padding across the hall. The back door was opened and shut quietly. The only sound now was of water dripping into the basin over his head.

HENRY CADWALLADER THORNE
23rd December

H E SHIFTED THE FLASHLIGHT so that its yellow eye traveled over the body lying in the bed. The corpse set in rigor mortis had been difficult to strip — even more difficult to dress in a pair of his own silk pajamas. He pulled up the sheet, leaving the head and arms free, looking at the open staring eyes with a sense of triumph. He'd beaten them all at their own game, and this was the moment of victory.

He set the bedside table with an assortment of objects. The sort of things a man empties from his pockets late at night. A handkerchief, a pen and pencil set, money — a silver lighter engraved with the initials H.C.T. A suit with a tailor's label bearing his name hung over a nearby chair.

A floorboard creaked in the corridor. He snapped the light off, listening to the sound of his own breathing in the darkness. Gradually he relaxed, remembering other nights when the house seemed to stir with life of its own. His plan had been resolved for him.

The fire would start downstairs with Cameron the

obvious culprit. Inevitably the police and the fire brigade would come up with theories of their own as to how it all started. A match dropped by a man who'd had too much to drink — a perverse draft creating a flashback in the central-heating system. The trail he had laid ensured a quick spread of flames to both the furnace room and the second story. The pine paneling and flooring would ignite within minutes. A couple of open windows would provide oxygen to boost the flames. He'd watch from the woods till he was sure that the fire was beyond control. Whoever was first on the scene would find a burned-out shell of a house and a couple of cremated skeletons. He could call the police from a safe distance — announcing himself as the same anonymous informant who'd given them the original lead. When they were done with their measuring and photographing nothing in the world would stop them from identifying one of the bodies as Bruce Cameron. It followed by logic and suggestion that the second was George Watson alias Henry Thorne. Nothing had been left to chance. Chalice, his partner and the doctor were gagged by training and complicity. And Jamie would never be sure.

He picked up Cameron's suitcase and distributed the clothes in the next bedroom. Friends and comrades — they slept close together. He left the documents and Canadian passport in a silver box where they might well be found or the burned fragments at least deciphered. He made his way downstairs, avoiding the oil-soaked bed linen that linked the upstairs corridor with the furnace room. He tiptoed across the hall to the cloakroom and listened. After a while he turned away satisfied.

His dufflecoat was hanging in the kitchen. It was bitterly cold outside. The hairs in his nostrils stiffened. There was no moon. The only light there was came from the snow. He skirted the northern boundary wall till he came to the door leading to what had been a paddock. The back lane through the woods to the Warrens' house was completely obscured. The tracks made by Jamie and Chalice headed in the direction of the main highway, three miles distant. He started to climb the hill, aiming at the heart of the woods. It was heavy going. Fresh powder snow lay on top of yesterday's frozen crust. It packed on his soles, forcing him to stop every fifty yards or so and free himself of the encumbrance. Once into the forest it was easier going. The white-shrouded oaks had acted as buffers, taking the force of the weather. Here the snow lay thinner. It was possible to see the faint outline of the lane ahead. He walked faster, following the trail that looped through the trees. The hushed wood received him without sign of life. There was a static quality about everything — as if the scene were held permanently in the hard grip of winter. Yet he'd walked here only a few short weeks ago with the night wind whipping the branches, sending leaves scurrying in the shadows. He'd heard a fox bark, the raucous alarm of a carrion crow.

He forded the stream at the bottom of the hill,

slithering from one stepping stone to another. The water ran turbulently, its course narrowed by the encroaching ice. He stepped onto the far bank and lowered the hood of his coat, sensing movement behind him. A branch bent low, releasing a cascade of snow. He nodded to himself, alive to danger but well equipped to deal with it.

The forest ended abruptly, hedged in by post and rail fencing. The trail vanished again, lost somewhere in the white-blanketed fields lying ahead. He climbed the fence and slithered down the slope towards the lights at the bottom. The house lay two hundred yards away, a low brick building surrounded by formal gardens. Behind it were the stables and yard. He approached them cautiously, anticipating the challenge of the dogs. It came as he entered the yard. A pair of lurchers bounded out, yellow eyed and long legged. They investigated him silently then one of them bayed. A dog inside the house howled in sympathy. He bent for a stone. The lurchers retreated to a safe distance, still baying. He cut across the lighted yard.

The cobblestone had been cleared of snow and covered with a straw circle. Dung and hoofmarks showed where horses had been exercised. He passed close to a loose-box, smelling the warm spicy air inside. A chestnut colt poked its head over the top of the door, ears flattened. A youth crossed the yard, calling off the dogs. Thorne nodded at him and took the swept brick path round to the front of the house. The drawing room curtains were tightly closed. He lifted the foxhead doorknocker and scraped the muck from his shoes. A dog barked hysterically. The door was thrown open.

Colonel Warren was in his late sixties with the build of a cavalryman. He had neat white hair and bright eyes, skin the color of a saddle. He was wearing baggy corduroy trousers and a checked flannel shirt. His eyes widened as he recognized his caller.

"Good God, if it isn't Watson! What brings *you* here? I hadn't even heard that you were down. As a matter of fact, I thought it was the vicarage squad again. You know — three bars of 'Hark the Herald Angels,' and the buggers want money. They've been here twice already. Come on in."

He led the way through a hall bristling with regimental photographs. The drawing room furniture and carpet were old but handsome. The bole of a small apple tree burned in the open fireplace. An asthmatic pug heaved itself up from a cushion and launched itself at Thorne's ankles, yelping. The Colonel put a slippered foot under its tail. He straightened his leg, lifting it into the hall with the ease of practice. He shut the door firmly.

"Let me get you something to take the chill out of your bones. How long are you down for?"

"Just over Christmas," said Thorne. "I came with a friend."

Warren cocked his lean head as if he were still on the parade ground. He looked at the lump on Thorne's chin.

Thorne touched it self-consciously. "Chopping wood to light the fire. A piece flew up in my face. I wondered if I could borrow your Landrover, Colonel. My car's stuck in a drift and I've got to go over to Templecombe to collect something."

Warren's face brightened with anticipation. "Of course you can. I'll tell you what, I'll come in with you. Some fresh air'll do me good. You did say sherry, didn't you?"

He poured a glass of wine for Thorne, opened the door and bawled upstairs.

"It's Mr. Watson, Joanna. Mr. *Watson* from over the hill! His car's stuck. I'm going to run him into Templecombe."

He closed his eyes as a formidable voice boomed in answer. "It's no good shouting — I can't hear a thing. I'm coming down."

Sturdy heels clattered down the stairs. Mrs. Warren marched into the drawing room, the pug following with new-found confidence. She was almost as tall as her husband and even more angular. Her dress appeared to have been cut out of some mediocre curtain material. She wore a switch of defiantly ginger hair attached to a velvet band. She turned a cold stare on Thorne and made no secret of its result.

"Was that *you* wandering about in the stableyard?"

Thorne smiled ingratiatingly. "I'm afraid so. I walked over through the woods. I hope I didn't alarm you."

She fitted a cigarette into a long holder, showing teeth that seemed to be fashioned from bone splinters.

"I can assure you that I'm not that easily alarmed,

Mr. Watson. I gather you don't keep horses. Otherwise you'd know they're better undisturbed at feed time. Did I understand you to say 'walked'?"

He moved his head in assent. "My car's stuck. I was telling your husband."

She waved her cigarette holder. "Is your telephone out of order too?"

Warren cleared his throat. "I'm going to run him over to Templecombe in the Landrover."

Thorne put his glass down. The Colonel's company was the last thing he wanted. Mrs. Warren came to his aid, unexpectedly but firmly. "You're doing no such thing, Roger. I want to talk to you about something. Added to which I refuse to be left in this house alone again."

Warren's tone was patient. "There are four people on the premises. You can hardly call that being left alone."

Her glare scotched the attempt at mild humor. "I can see absolutely no reason for you going. I'm sure Mr. Watson's quite capable of driving himself to Templecombe and back. But do as you want, of course. You usually do. Good *night*, Mr. Watson!" She left, taking the snuffling dog with her.

Warren drained his glass. He turned the log in the fireplace. "Well, that's that," he said with his back turned. "Are you married?"

"No," said Thorne.

Warren nodded as if confirmed in some secret thought. He fished a set of car keys from a drawer and gave them to Thorne.

"You're quite sure you can manage alone? I can send one of the boys with you if you like."

Thorne stood up. "Positive." He hesitated. "I was wondering whether I could have a word with you in confidence, Colonel."

Wariness flitted across the Colonel's face — the wariness of a man who senses that a favor is going to be asked of him.

"Yes," he said noncommittally.

Thorne squared his shoulders. The impression he had to give was of someone in desperate need of a confidant. A man trapped by circumstance, frightened and on the verge of avowal.

"I don't really know how to start," he said.

Colonel Warren's keen glance sought the heart of the matter. His smile was understanding.

"A woman? It generally is, isn't it?"

Thorne made a small resigned gesture. "I'm afraid it isn't as simple as that, sir. The fact is that I've got myself into a bit of a mess." He stopped, chin up but reluctant to continue.

Warren put both hands behind him and paced back into a world of order and discipline. Bugles rang. Sentries were posted round the horse lines. He was facing a junior officer with a problem across the dying campfire.

"Don't rush your fences," he said weightily. "Look here, why don't you come over for Christmas dinner? Bring your friend. We'd be glad to have your company. We can have a chat together then."

Thorne started to button up his coat. The Colonel

sat on the local bench of magistrates. He was a friend of the Chief Constable. He imagined the ex-soldier taking command of the situation, repeating his story till memory glossed fact with fiction.

Of course, I knew the feller. He'd moved into the district and appeared to be a gentleman. You know — one has a feeling about these things. As a matter of fact he came over to borrow my Landrover the night before it happened. I can remember thinking then that there was something odd about his behavior. I had a sort of — "premonition," I suppose you'd call it. But I'll be quite frank. I was completely taken in by the chap. You can understand how I felt when I heard the news — entertaining a crook on the run in one's house!

"I'd be very glad to come, sir," Thorne said quietly.

"Excellent." Warren led the way through a pass door, through the kitchens and into the stableyard. He stepped out in slippered feet, looking up at the sky and shaking his head. "The weather people say we've got another week of this, at least. You'd better keep the Landrover over at your place. You'll need it on Christmas Day. By the way — were you out with a gun about an hour or so ago?"

The Colonel's face was guileless in the light from the hanging lamp. Thorne shook his head.

"Me? No. I'm a fisherman. I wouldn't know one end of a gun from the other. Why do you ask?"

Colonel Warren pulled on a pair of overshoes, grunting. "It certainly sounded as though it came from your direction. There was something odd about the report. In fact, I'd have sworn it was a pistol shot. But one's ears can play tricks. Would you like to look at the horses?"

He switched on a light in one of the loose-boxes. A bay horse spun round, white eyed and nickering. Warren fondled its ears, avoiding its playful nip.

Thorne's tongue felt solid. "Christmas Day if I may. I really think I ought to get a move on. I'm not sure what time the station closes."

Warren switched the light off, his face thoughtful. "It just might have been a twenty-two, though what one would be doing out in this weather with a twenty-two God alone knows. One of those hooligans from West Wellow, in all probability. The rot's struck there, you know. We've got it in the village — the long hair, winklepicker shoes. The lot. I'm just waiting for one of them to come up on a charge in front of me. Let's see if you've got enough petrol."

The pair of lurchers joined them in the garage, tails thudding against the big Jaguar parked next to the Landrover. Warren opened the yard gate.

"Well, so long then. We'll expect you on Christmas Day." He lifted a hand in salute as the Landrover ploughed into the deep snow on the driveway. Everything was falling into line. One thing was sure, he must be careful about using the gun. Not that it was necessary. Cameron would be dead before the rope was untied, his head shoved into the oven with the burners on fullblast. He'd last twenty minutes, a half hour, no more certainly. The headlamps picked out the churchyard wall, striking light from the stained-glass windows. Children bundled into coats, scarves and woolen caps were building a snowman on the green. They waved, seeing the Landrover. He leaned out and waved back. Let them *all* remember him.

There was little traffic on the road. A white-coated maintenance crew was salt-sanding the surface at the junction with the main highway. The Weston cutoff and the bridge hemmed in a deep vee of beech trees where Chalice and Jamie must have waited to be picked up. They'd be halfway back to London by now, congratulating themselves at being well out of an unpleasant situation. He moved the car forward as the foreman waved him on. He took the north road that cut across country to Templecombe.

The station approach was bare of the usual complement of parked cars. Lamps behind the iron railings shone on stretches of empty track. Through the window of the waiting room he could see a few passengers huddled round the stove. The buffet and newsstand were locked, bolted and shuttered, adding the last touch of inflexible inhospitality. He backed up as near as he could to the entrance to the parcels office. The oil-fired room was warm and stuffy. A red-faced man with dusty overalls and a porter's cap said good evening.

Thorne pushed the bill of lading at him. "I can see it from here. That tea chest in front of the motorcycle."

The porter moved across the room with bucolic economy of movement.

"One of the lucky ones. From what they say up the

line, there's stuff'll be weeks late. You'll be the gel-man as phoned this morning, I reckon?"

He made a cursory check of the labels and dragged the case over to the door. He mopped his face, pan-tomiming exhaustion. He looked at the Landrover and nodded.

"Not much else as would get you back to Weston tonight, is there, sir, though they do say the main roads has been cleared. Colonel Warren's, isn't it?"

Thorne lowered the tailgate. They heaved the case up into the back of the vehicle. He pushed some coins into the porter's hand. The man showed bad teeth.

"Thank you, sir. And a Merry Christmas."

Thorne started the motor, not moving till the por-ter was safely in his office. The wing mirror reflected an empty booking hall, snow-covered cottage gardens backing onto the station approach. There was no charge from the shadows — not even a solitary blast on a policeman's whistle. The irony was that this part of the plan had worked perfectly. He thought sud-denly of Seager, tramping about in his Bayswater flat, doing his best to convince himself that his money was safe. He'd turn up on Monday as arranged, eleven o'clock, sitting on a bench by the Serpentine, waiting for Robin to appear with five thousand pounds in a paper package. Another fool who'd swallowed more than his stomach could digest.

The lights were still on in Weston church. He heard the organ long before he reached the green, the bellowing of a carol. They'd have something more exciting to occupy their minds before the next twenty-four hours were out. He turned into his own lane and dropped into first gear. The heavy vehicle crept forward pressing broad tracks in the loose powdery snow. He unhooked the gate at the end of the lane. The house had lost all form. The only point of reference was the firelight flickering behind the sitting room curtains. He took the steel towrope from the back of the Landrover and attached it to the towbar. The Austin was hub deep in churned up snow. He sprung the handbrake and buckled the free end of the hawser round the front bumper.

He climbed back in the Landrover and let the clutch in slowly. The towrope snapped taut. The four-wheel drive found purchase. The Landrover surged forward, dragging the minicar behind it. He stopped at the gates and changed vehicles, unhitching the towrope. The Austin caught at the first push of the starting button. He drove to the end of the lane and back, keeping to the tracks he'd made with the Landrover. The small car tended to spin but it was still maneuverable. He parked it by the gate and went back to the Landrover. He broke open the tea chest with a tire lever. The long trip had left the contents undisturbed. He plunged both hands deep into the box till his fingers met the waxy feel of banknotes. What he really ought to do was bring Cameron outside, force him to load the loot into the Austin.

He took the back seat from the Austin and laid it on the ground. There was enough space around the upholstery springs to stow half the money. The rest he packed in the suitcase that lay there ready and locked it in the trunk. He could find a better hiding place for it later. He'd be first on the lineup for the early morning ferry and the hell with its destination. Calais, Boulogne, Dunkirk, Ostend. Anywhere out of England.

The police would be looking for a name not a face. Thorne certainly. Possibly Watson. Turberville never. At this time of the year the ferries were underbooked. A couple of quid in the right hand would make certain of a berth.

There was nothing to fear from customs and excise inspection. It was negligible on the outward journey. Most of the routine work was left to representatives of the automobile clubs. One of these would check the car's identification. Two hours afterwards he'd be in Normandy. The car could be left in a garage to rot. He'd take a plane to Paris. One thing he must remember to do in the morning was phone the bank and cancel his letter.

He stared up at the house. There was no real reason to wait till early morning. The fire couldn't be seen from the village. It couldn't be seen from anywhere except the air. If he set light to the place now, he'd be in Dover by midnight. He pulled his gloves back on and started up the driveway. He was almost into the porch when he stopped dead and swung round trying to locate a danger he only sensed. He saw, heard and smelled nothing. Suddenly footsteps broke in the opposite direction, down the drive towards the cars. He wrenched the back door open and ran into the house, gun in hand.

BRUCE CAMERON

23rd December

H E WAS LYING with his left shoulder pressed against the floor. A cold draft blowing under the door made his eyes water. The pattern of sound in his ears hadn't varied for an hour. There was the same gurgle from the stream running under the house, snow shifting on the heated roof, the creaking of the kitchen window. It was a long while before he made his first move, suspicious still of a trap. Everything suggested that Thorne had really left the house — probably to collect the packing case. He might well have been telling the truth about the Landrover.

He rolled over till his head touched the wall. He tried to raise his body, using his shoulder and knee as levers. The rope cut into his throat cruelly. He overbalanced, falling heavily. He wormed his way to the chair in front of the mirror, nudged it into a corner and tried again. He leaned his chest on the chair, taking the weight off his legs. He struggled into a squatting position, heels pressing into his buttocks. His wrists were only inches away from them. The rope slackened, easing the pressure on his throat. He gulped air through an open mouth, sweat running down his ribs. He was able to move his fingers, his wrists with difficulty. He tilted himself backwards, gaining precious inches of slack. Now his fingers were touching the bottoms of his shoes. He picked at the soles, searching for the leather plugs. He pulled out the first, then the second, third and fourth. He twisted the flanged screws and pulled the soles off. The package of hacksaw blades was in the left shoe. He tore one free of its greased-paper wrappings. Holding the blade between his thumbs, he lifted his buttocks till the serrated edge of the blade was pressing against the rope round his ankles. He started rocking backwards and forwards. The rope gave suddenly. He scrambled up, collapsing on the chair as the blood began to circulate freely. He sat for a while, hands still knotted behind his back, holding the blade. The rope was looped round his throat, passing down between his shoulder blades to his wrists. He could move his hands upwards and sideways. The blade went through the rope in seconds. He undid the last knot, filled the basin with cold water and plunged his head into it. A band tightened round his temples, freeing his brain.

He mopped his dripping head with a towel. He was in there with a chance whatever came next. A faint glint showed through the keyhole. He turned the handle, throwing his full weight against the door. It was solid and resisted his assault. He poked the end of the hacksaw blade into the space between the door and the frame, feeling for the tongue of the lock. It went in an inch then the jamb blocked it. He opened the window wide. The bars set in the ledge were about six inches apart. He wiped the snow from the end bar.

A rough hoop of laurels and rhododendrons circled the lawn. One arm stretched out towards the stable-yard, the other curved in the direction of the front driveway. Beyond the belt of shrubbery lay darkness. He wrapped both ends of the blade in lavatory paper and went to work. He sawed steadily, greasing the cut with soap he took from the wash basin. The high-speed steel bit into the bar with a harsh whine that seemed to fill the garden. The way he was standing, the lack of a frame made it difficult to hold the blade taut. He broke two blades making the first cut. He was halfway through the second when a new sound invaded his consciousness. He stopped sawing and listened. A car was coming up the lane from the village. Seconds later headlamps swept the back of the house, reaching deep into the obscurity. He had a brief impression of a wall, trees staggered on a hill, then the lights went out.

He took hold of the bottom of the bar with both hands, bracing his knees against the wall. The bar came back slowly till it was at right angles to the window ledge. He scrambled through the aperture, throwing out both hands as he fell. He landed in a heap in a clump of chrysanthemums. As he picked himself up, he realized that he'd left his shoes in the cloakroom. He raced across the grass into the shrubbery and worked himself deep into the bushes. His feet made no sound but the tangled branches betrayed

225

every movement he made. He forced on blindly for a dozen yards till he was snagged by thorns. He tore himself from their grasp and tried to fix his position. The outline of the barn told him that he'd rounded the end of the house. Anything more precise he couldn't tell. He stretched his hands out, feeling thick impenetrable branches. He dropped down on his knees. Water was running somewhere off to the left. He crawled towards it. The stream followed the line of the driveway, north-south under the house. Dead nettles poked from the snow, stinging his hands and face.

He was determined that nothing would stop him. He had no thought of escape any more, no thought of Jamie — nothing beyond the knowledge of what he had to do. Light swept the bushes in front of him. He flattened himself on his stomach, inching away. The Landrover was twenty yards down the drive, Thorne in the driving seat. He watched it lurch forward, hauling the minicar out of the drift on the end of a towrope. He lay quite still, conscious now of agonizing cold in his feet.

Thorne changed cars. The Austin disappeared up the lane. Cameron slithered a few feet nearer the Landrover. The tailgate was down. He could just make out the shape of the packing case. He retreated hastily as the Austin reappeared. Thorne stopped it in the middle of the driveway and climbed out. He carried an armful of money from the back of the Landrover to the car, stowing the bundles in the springing of the seat. The rest he put in a suitcase. There was enough light from the lamps to see his face. He was smiling as he walked towards the house.

Cameron moved out of the bushes, a dim shape on the edge of the gravel. Thorne was walking like a man with all the time in the world, completely sure of himself. But as he reached the porch doorway he spun round. He leaned forward, stifling a cough, searching the darkness. He turned and ran into the house, slamming the door behind him.

Cameron bolted down the drive, skidding the last few yards. He yanked the ignition keys from both cars and sprinted towards the stableyard. Lights were coming on in the house — the kitchen, the hall, the sitting room. He stuffed both sets of keys into the open end of a drainpipe and ducked into the toolshed.

The floor was littered with ploughshares, harrows and drills. He sat on a roller and rubbed some feeling back into his feet. He got up stiffly and headed for the end of the shed. There was a jacket he'd noticed earlier, hanging on the wall. It was fouled by birds, nibbled by mice, but at least a layer of wool that would insulate him against the cold. He tied it round his waist with string. He dug among a heap of sacks till he found the one he wanted. He cut it into strips with a sickle and wrapped his feet in lengths of burlap.

He walked to the door, taking the sickle with him. It was heavy enough to wield as a weapon, light enough to throw with precision. He worked his way round to the barn, keeping close to the wall. It didn't matter about the prints he was making in the snow.

To see them, Thorne would have to make tracks of his own. He trotted through the barn. The willows and laurels were thick on the banks of the stream. The house was in darkness. Suddenly he heard somebody at the cars. A motor turned without firing. He ran, hoping to outflank Thorne before he could get back to the house. He was nowhere near the tiny bridge. The stream was six feet wide, the banks treacherous with rat holes. He grabbed an overhanging branch and swung out, landing high on the other side. Two shots followed in rapid succession. The shells whined into the undergrowth. The noise of the explosions lingered in the distant woods. Snow slithered from the branches, plopping into the flashing water. The silence that followed was almost tangible. The sound of Thorne pounding back up the driveway broke it.

Cameron lost valuable seconds in the dense bushes. He was thirty yards away as the back door was slammed and bolted. He sprinted round to the front. The door there was locked. He managed to hurl himself sideways just in time. Two more shells smacked through the wood where he had been standing. He flattened himself against the wall and tipped away in the opposite direction. Only a course of brickwork separated him from the downstairs corridor. He had an unpleasant feeling that Thorne was matching steps with him inside.

He picked up a rock and hurled it at the nearest window. He was gone in the same second, running for the shelter of the laurels. He squatted there, the sickle across his legs. A faint movement caught his eye. A hand holding the gun came through the broken window, swinging from side to side like a snake's head. He projected his voice through cupped hands.

"You've got three shells. And I've got the car keys. You're going *no*where!"

More glass shattered as the gun swung towards him. It barked once more then Thorne's footsteps thudded up the stairs.

Cameron covered the ground to the window at a steady walk. He climbed through into the hall corridor. Light came from the sitting room fire. All the doors were open. Bed linen littered the floor and the stairs. There was a strong smell of kerosene. He started up the stairs, holding the sickle over his shoulder. He was halfway to the top when the lights came on. Thorne was waiting on the landing, legs splayed, the gun sighted at Cameron's head.

"Throw me the car keys, Bruce," he said hoarsely. "It's your only chance."

The sickle dropped from Cameron's grasp, bounced a couple of times and landed in the hall. His eyes never left Thorne's face.

"You're wrong," he said. "I'm going to show you you're wrong."

Thorne retreated till he reached the open doorway. He stopped there, his face bloodless.

"We'll split. Half the money for a set of car keys."

He made the last long step, meeting the bullet with his left shoulder. He spun under the force of its impact. His good hand found the wall, stopping him from collapsing. He looked with wonder at the blood soaking his sleeve and hauled himself very slowly forward.

Thorne's move was quicker. He jabbed the barrel of the gun into his mouth and pulled the trigger. The back of his skull seemed to jump. His arms dropped to his sides. He stood for one hideous second, blood running from his head, nose and mouth, then fell backwards on the bed behind him.

Cameron staggered into the bathroom. He padded a towel and pushed it under his shirt. He clenched his left fist and held it tightly against his chest. The bleeding seemed to slow. Thorne was lying across the bed, his back resting against Gunn's body. Cameron dragged his eyes away. The slightest movement required a major decision. Each step down to the hall was a towering cliff that somehow had to be negotiated. He leaned heavily on the banisters, leaving a trail of blood on the bed linen cluttering the stairs.

The fire had burned low, putting the room in deep shadow. He swayed in the doorway, eyes blurring. Five more steps to the bookcase. Telephone. No dial. Just lift it off the stand. He watched his hand on its long weary journey. The operator's inquiry roared into his ears.

"Police," he whispered then his voice slid away. He reached gratefully into the enveloping darkness.

>>> If you've enjoyed this book and would like to discover more great vintage crime and thriller titles, as well as the most exciting crime and thriller authors writing today, visit: >>>

The Murder Room
Where Criminal Minds Meet

themurderroom.com